# Dippin' My Spoon

# Dippin' My Spoon

*by*

NINA FOXX

**Manisy Willows Books**

Austin, Texas

Manisy Willows Books
701 Capital of Texas Highway, Box 1202
Austin, Texas 78746
Copyright © 2000 by Nina Foxx.

Book Design by BW Design, Inc.
Cover Design by Kim Greyer Graphic Design.
Cover Illustration by John Ashford.
Edited by Norma Martin.

ISBN 0-7394-1793-2

*For my Husband, Major,*
*Who enjoys letting me be me.*

*And for my daughter, Sydney,*
*Who is just learning to do her own thang, ya'll.*

*In memory of my parents,*
*Brison Browne Solon Hamilton III,*
*And Elvie Jackson,*
*Who gave me such fantastic tools.*

# Acknowledgments

This was a big project, and I would not have been able to complete it without the love and support of my wonderful family and friends. Thank God for all of them. Maj, you are wonderful. Have you read it yet? Charlenne, thanks for becoming a great Mom-In-Law. Lynda, Robert & Brandie, you guys are the bestest!

Thanks to Pam Lipp and Jill Hubley (no, girlies, it ain't about you. That's the next book!). You were my first readers and you didn't laugh out loud. Shia Shabazz Barnett, girl, you are so talented. Thank you for inspiring me to take care of business. Maurice, thanks to you too. You asked the magic question that pushed me over the edge and made me step out there.

Toinette Holmes and Michelle Ewell, thanks for being my homies. Sharon, Thank you for decorating my life and my home. Norma, girl, you pulled it together. I owe you big time.

Kwame Alexander, you added so much structure and direction. Thanks for being the best publishing consultant any person could have.

To all of my sorors of Alpha Kappa Alpha Sorority, Inc., in both Austin and Phoenix, – You are wonderful. Thank you for your unending support and sisterliness. You are a prime example of the magic of our organization. I will always proudly wear my pearls.

Finally, thank you to the readers, without you, there would be no book! One Love.

# 1

AMBER LAREAUX SLUMPED in her chair as the woman in her office droned on and on.

Lynette sucked her teeth, glaring in Amber's general direction.

"I said, what do you think that means?"

Amber wasn't listening. In fact, she hadn't been listening for several months.

"I'm sorry, Lynette. Let's end here."

Amber's answer was brusque. Her detached manner would have been obvious to any normal person; it was even obvious to Lynette. Amber was slouched down in her chair and had not made eye contact with Lynette in over 20 minutes.

Amber sighed. It was no use trying to listen to her client's problems; her heart just wasn't in it. She stood and walked toward the door, giving Lynette her cue to leave.

Lynette sucked her teeth again, but this time she stood up, rolling her eyes as she did. Amber smiled, guiding Lynette through the door, trying to make her false empathy appear real. She knew Lynette would forget the whole thing as soon as the doctor okayed her prescription refill. That was really what she had come for anyway, not to speak with Amber.

Amber worked in a community mental health center as a case manager. Originally, she thought she wanted to be a clinical psychologist; what else do you do with a psychology degree? So she got a position in a clinic as a case manager for people released from the state psychiatric facility but too poor to afford expensive psychiatric or psychological help. She saw most of her clients once a month and listened to their problems before they got to see the psychiatrist. Graduate programs in clinical psychology looked favorably upon that type of experience in their admissions process. Several of the other case managers were graduate interns.

To Amber's surprise, she hated her job. In fact, she felt like telling most of her clients to wake up and get a life or a job, sometimes both. Instead of being inspired to apply to graduate school in clinical psychology, Amber found herself steering toward industrial psychology. She was more interested in the dynamics between the workers in her office; she was more interested in what motivated her peers than she was in what was going on inside the head of her clients, even if those ailments actually had a real name attached to them.

From her window, Amber watched as Lynette waited for the bus. She was a classic case of what bored Amber about her job. The psychiatrist said Lynette was depressed. Sure Lynette had problems, but who didn't? Amber was depressed too. She was married to a husband who she wasn't sure she really loved anymore; she worked in a job she hated, but she didn't sit around and cry about it all day.

With a deep breath and then a long exhale, Amber turned and picked up her briefcase, asking herself how long it would be before she moved on. She knew she couldn't do this much longer.

Some people got a kick out of being stalked by their clients or talking a 14 year-old girl out of committing suicide, but not her. She felt she was living in an on-going episode of some TV docu-drama. She hadn't told anyone that she was already applying to doctoral programs in industrial psychology, none of which were local. The sad part was Amber hadn't even told her husband yet.

She tidied up her office, preparing to leave for the day. She knew the battle with Tyler would be a tough one, but she had made up her mind that today would be the day. He probably wouldn't even hear her over the blare of his television set. She was sure he would be sitting right where she left him this morning. Lately it was as if his butt had somehow grown roots that attached him to the sofa. Amber thought about her upcoming conversation with Tyler during the drive from her office to her house.  It was definitely time for a discussion, only she didn't know what to say.

# 2

IT WAS WARM IN AUSTIN, as it almost always was, even though it was technically winter. Amber glanced at her watch, realizing she had been daydreaming in the car for 15 minutes. The air in the car had become stifling; the ignition was off and the dirty windows on the car were still rolled up.

Amber sat staring at the clouds; they were grayish and low, with the sun peeking through at various intervals. It looked sort of like it might storm. Her grandmother would have said she wasn't daydreaming, but procrastinating, thinking of ways to avoid facing her husband.

Amber continued to sit in the parking lot of her Lake Hills

apartment complex, west of Austin. She and her husband had lived on the edge of Yuppie-ville for a couple of years now. She began to feel the sweat forming between her pantyhose and skin; it was creeping through to the outside of her dress. It made her skin crawl as it snapped her out of her daydream and back to reality. Amber knew she would have to shower immediately; wet pantyhose and sweat equaled funk with a capital "F".

Getting out of her car, she sighed and she made the short walk to her apartment door. Turning the key in the lock, she could already hear the television set blaring through the door. She opened the door confronting the scene she knew she would find.

As usual, Tyler was sitting on the sofa in his underwear. If he stood, Amber knew she would see his dingy briefs, sagging in the butt with a yellow stain in the front.

She passed the sofa on her way to the bedroom, disgusted by Tyler's inactivity; she had been subjected to the same scene many times recently. Her hello was perfunctory. Tyler was oblivious to Amber and her attitude at the moment; he was absorbed in his TV show playing on the beat-up television set.

Amber knew it was time for her to talk to Tyler. She was just beginning to know herself better and realized it was now or never. If she didn't say something to Tyler soon, she would lose her courage and it would be easy for him to push her into being defensive about her decisions. Instead of changing her clothes, she joined Tyler on the sofa, funky pantyhose and all; she didn't even wait for a commercial.

"Honey, I think I want to go to graduate school."

Her voice had no hint of the tentativeness she was feeling. Only the tissue in her hand showed her nervousness; it wasn't even used, yet it was falling apart as Amber twisted it over and over, wrapping it around and through her long, slender fingers. She nudged him as she spoke; if she didn't, he wouldn't hear her. To Amber's surprise, Tyler answered her on the first try, without turning his head to look in her direction.

"You're already in graduate school."

His mouth was full of nachos, making it hard for him to talk. He continued to stare at the television screen. Amber sighed and was kinda glad he didn't look at her; Nacho breath was a bitch. She contemplated her next words.

Amber watched the two people on TV along with Tyler; they were about to come to blows and from the corner of her eye she could see the talk show bouncer-goons readying themselves off to the side. The wrong response and she knew she would lose Tyler's attention altogether. She was glad he answered but was again feeling the familiar stir of disgust; Tyler's crumbs were everywhere and she was going to have to vacuum the floor. She was even sitting on crumbs; her thighs itched where her pantyhose met the sofa.

Amber was enrolled in school already; that much was true. But a master's degree in clinical psychology wasn't going to do it. She knew Tyler probably had never even heard of industrial psychology but Amber was prepared to explain. Hell, every time she mentioned it to anyone, the only thing anyone heard was 'psychology'. Most people made comments about reading minds or analyzing people or something.

Amber's response now was practiced in anticipation of Tyler's questions. She simplified down to a short mush about studying people in organizations and productivity; she was prepared to break it down for Tyler if he asked.

An Oil of Olay commercial broke Tyler's electronic trance. He usually used commercial time to channel surf but instead of picking up the remote, he continued to answer Amber.

"Where are you going to get the money for all this?"

They had been together for what seemed like forever, but it was obvious to Amber that her husband thought he was not obligated to help her pay for school or anything else. Amber wasn't surprised he focused on money, he always did. The first major fight of their married life was about money. Although they both had jobs, the fight that began because Tyler felt all of the money in their joint checking account belonged to him.

Amber didn't take the bait. Tyler's mouth was cocked to the side in his "what-the-hell-are-you-talking-about" scowl, telling her he wanted a fight. She didn't want to take the bait. Not this time.

"It's not the money I am worried about. That's the easy part. The money will come."

He always brought up the money argument, but Amber wasn't going there this time; she refused to be sidetracked. The commercials were over anyway.

There was no use trying to discuss this with Tyler while some angry audience member was screaming at the panel guest. Amber rolled her eyes and wondered where the nuts on these shows came from.

"Why do Black people have to be so colorful?'" she thought. She watched as the woman's head rolled around on her shoulders, but she didn't hear her angry words. It was obvious that Tyler didn't think her going to graduate school was a good idea. He was already back to concentrating on his show and had not offered one encouraging word. If it required money, he always thought it was a bad idea, especially if it involved her. She knew this because she knew him. They had been together for ten years now, and the entire time after they graduated from college, she followed him. After a decade of following him through four states, Amber knew Tyler well.

Tyler didn't like the idea because he would have to follow her for a change. He wanted to be the provider and it was not "manly" for him to shape his career plans around her. It was bad enough that they lived down in Austin instead of Killeen, closer to the military base, so Amber could get a better job. The original deal they made was they would attend college, and when he was done, he would spend the time that his R.O.T.C. scholarship required of him in the military. Then, it would be Amber's turn to do what she needed to do.

Amber was young, naive, and in love when she made that

deal. Now Tyler's time in the military was almost up; the required 6 years had been cut short. Amber's patience was growing short. The time had come for the shoe to be on the other foot. Over the past couple of months, Amber couldn't help thinking about making the arrangement with Tyler way back when. She thought about it all the time, and as she did, all she could do was ask herself when was it going to be her turn.

Amber and Tyler had been high school sweethearts. They met, when she was fifteen years old, in a high school economics class. Amber hadn't liked Tyler at first; he was very popular, and it had obviously gone to his head. Amber watched him strut around school with his barrel-chest stuck out and noticed the way he was always fashionably late to everything. Tyler would walk into every room like he wanted everyone to stop and take notice, and most of the time people did.

He made Amber's skin crawl, but she kept ending up sitting next to Tyler Montpelier because their names were next to each other in the alphabet. Even though they eventually got together, Amber never could stomach his surname. When they married she kept her maiden name, much to the dismay of Tyler's family, the Montpeliers. She would always be a LaReaux; Amber felt her father was the best man she would ever know.

Tyler was very competitive. The problem was he was competitive with Amber too. He would get bent out of shape if Amber's grades were even one point better than his were. The thing was, her grades always were better without her even trying.

Their economics teacher would hand the exams out in descending grade order, and Amber was always the first to receive hers back. Amber would often smirk as she watched Tyler's reaction. He was so obnoxious he didn't even try to hide his scowl.

Eventually, they did become friends. It was a group assignment in their economics class that finally brought them together. They were studying the stock market and invested imaginary money into some company their group had picked. Their assignment was to follow the stock for a semester. It was the beginning of the personal computer era, and their group had picked Apple Computer.

That stock was the only thing on which Amber and Tyler could agree. The then small company was listed at five dollars a share. Who knew that Apple Computer would take off like it did in the beginning? If only the money they invested were real! Their newly found imaginary wealth sparked a friendship. If Amber could have seen the future, she might have given Tyler her share of the booty and walked away. Amber often thought of Apple Computer as a metaphor for their life together; both the now troubled computer company and their relationship had seen better days.

The unexpected calm from the TV set bought Amber back to her present-day life. Glancing at the television, she realized there was a temporary lull in the fighting on the talk show Tyler was watching. She glanced over at him; he watched the television as if he were in some trance-like state. Amber pictured herself giving him a smack up side his head to get his attention. He always paid attention when people smacked each other on his talk shows.

After the Apple Computer incident, not only did Amber and Tyler become friends; they soon became THE couple of the high school. Every high school has the sort of couple who seems to be inseparable, joined at the hip. Always together, always happy. Tyler was very popular; he played football, won the lead in every school play since he was a freshman and even played in the high school jazz band. Amber, on the other hand, was not as popular or out-going. She was just smart, not a trait exactly praised by her peers. In fact, she hated high school. And to top it off, Amber was kinda shy. Amber had started school early and then skipped a grade, so she was younger than most of her classmates by almost two years, so she felt as if she were a misfit, more out of place than a square peg in a round hole.

Despite their differences, Amber and Tyler started dating anyway, in their senior year. During that year, and those that followed, there was ample opportunity for them to break up, but they stayed together, sort of like old shoes that you know need to be thrown away, but you keep them anyway hoping they will come back into style.

After they graduated, Amber attended a local college. At sixteen, there was no way in hell her family was going to let her live on campus, even in the same city. Tyler, on the other hand, went away to school. His parents didn't have money to pay for an expensive education, so he decided to get attend college out of town on an R.O.T.C. scholarship.

The years they spent in college proved to be rather bumpy for their relationship. The main problem was that Tyler went away to school and Amber didn't. He always knew what Amber was doing and who she was doing it with, and he often used the information to his advantage, saving it up until he needed it. In the middle of a fight, he would drop the bomb.

"I didn't say anything while you were stepping out to the thus-and-such with so-and-so." He always had details. He used this technique again and again to draw the blame back into Amber's corner.

This meant that Amber and Tyler fought often. She never knew when he dated other people, and he made her think he never even thought about doing it. The funny thing was Amber never figured out what he was doing until many years later.

Tyler never let on that someone was spying on Amber all those years until after they were married. He was so good at his spying that Amber still came home every day to sit in Tyler's nacho crumbs without ever knowing who his secret agent had been.

They stayed together through all of the ups and downs, and finally, in his senior year of college, Tyler asked Amber to marry him. Everyone expected them to get married anyway. They had been dating for nearly five years at that point, and soon they would have their college degrees. Since it was expected of them,

Amber agreed to get married. Actually, Amber always did what was expected of her although back then she didn't realize it. Besides, she liked the romance of getting married, even if she was more in love with being in love than she was with Tyler.

After they were married one week, Tyler had some surprises for her. His conscience got the best of him and he decided there was no better time to come clean. His choice of places to reveal his surprises wasn't the best. Tyler and Amber were meeting some friends for dinner at a trendy Chinese restaurant downtown, and just as the couple they were waiting for walked through the door, Tyler leaned over to Amber, smiling. Amber thought he was going to give her a kiss, instead he whispered, "Did I tell you that Kim says she is pregnant?"

Amber sucked in her breath. Kim was one of Tyler's flings who Amber knew about. He didn't have to say another word, she immediately knew that he meant that Kim was pregnant by him!

Tyler knew Amber well because he knew the one thing she would not do was make a scene in a public place. Time seemed to stand still for Amber as her friends approached the table. Amber produced the best smile she had in her and wore it all the way through that dinner. She asked for several napkins; she destroyed two with her never-ending napkin twisting before she got to use one for its intended purpose. She later found out that everyone else knew about the Tyler and Kim incident except her.

Tyler had been seeing Kim on and off for some time. He would invite her up to visit him at school often, usually when he was angry with Amber, where they would stay in a hotel. She was his long distance booty call. Tyler later told Amber he had forced Kim to have an abortion, but Amber wasn't sure she quite believed him. For all Amber knew, he could have a kid out running around somewhere.

Tyler had about three or four other stories that all involved other women, most of them people she knew. Tyler claimed Kim was the only one of them who had gotten pregnant. "So who else?" became a common mantra in their household. And all the time, during four years of college, he made her feel as if she were the bad one because she openly dated other people. But now they were married and the deal was made; she would follow him around for the next five years that he was to be in the military, and once it was over, he would follow her. How bad could it be?

They had been together seven years when they married. Now, three years later, Tyler's military career was ending, albeit a little earlier than he thought it would. It wasn't quite what he expected anyway, so why was he always so depressed?

While in R.O.T.C., Tyler believed that after graduation he would be special; the creme-de-la-creme of the armed forces. He would be a pilot and would get the best jobs. His hands would never get dirty because his education made him better than the average soldier. It didn't take long for him to discover what a crock that was! On his first assignment, Tyler was sent to the field in Germany for a whole month, right after they got married. And this wasn't just a stay-in-a-hotel-business-trip; it was really the field, complete with sleeping outside and the whole GI-Joe nine yards. And to top it off, when he returned, Tyler was in a car accident on the way to work. He was run off the road by a hit and run driver. His car hit a brick wall, leaving him with a head injury that caused him to be unable to fly. If that wasn't enough, he was also in a snowmobile accident that permanently damaged a ligament in his knee, making it even more impossible to keep up with the physical demands of his job. He would not be able to exercise or run the required two miles to prove that he was physically fit.

Tyler chose to leave the military early, and without consulting Amber, he was flying all over the country, interviewing for positions. Amber watched him pack for interview after interview and asked herself "what happened to my turn?" She had her own plans, and in those plans, her goals were top priority for a change.

But Tyler was old fashioned and competitive. He believed wives were supposed to follow their husbands, not vice versa. This was news to Amber; while they were dating he had led her to believe he felt marriage should be equal. The truth was he just could not stand to see Amber better herself in any manner. He was still the same competitive guy he had been back in high school.

Amber knew what Tyler was thinking, at least during the commercials. He was thinking he was already "letting" her get a master's degree in psychology, what more did she want? The scowl on his face made it obvious he was annoyed. He was also thinking she better be glad he was allowing her to make as many decisions as he was. At least he wasn't yelling and screaming.

Amber weighed her words. She knew her next suggestion was risky. She wanted Tyler to look for a job where she wanted to go to school.

"Tyler, have you thought about—"

"Do we have to discuss this now, during my talk show? You know this is my favorite!"

Tyler made eye contact with Amber for the first time since she had sat down on the sofa. Amber could see the annoyance on his face and knew it would be no use trying to continue talking to him.

"No, I guess not. It's not important."

She sighed as she stood up and headed toward the bedroom for a nap. The whole non-exchange with Tyler had left her tired.

# 3

FALLING ASLEEP IS ALWAYS THE SAME *for me; it feels like falling backward. I can feel it now; the wind is rushing upward as I fall backwards into blackness. It always amazes me when I think about how real it feels, even when I end up in the same places almost every night. Tonight is no different, I begin to feel the familiar lift as the hands lift me up. I feel like I am floating on top of a sea of people, but I can't see anything.*

*Drums are beating and I feel warm and not afraid as I move over the tops of hands. The mass of hands moves me toward the drums and I realize that people are singing along. In my mind I can see as the hands place me, upright, onto a podium. My eyes are still not working, but I know that people are crowded around the podium, most of them writhing in time with the drums.*

They are singing about Damballah as I reach out and let my hands be guided to remove the top of the straw basket that has been placed in front of me. I wonder where my eyes have gone. I sense that I am blind but no matter; I feel warm and am brimming with eagerness, and I realize there is a snake inside the basket. We are old friends. He, too, is moving to the drumbeat.

Somehow, I know the words as the crowd sings out, almost with perfect harmony. I can tell that this is not intended. No one has stood around and told sopranos to sing one thing and altos to sing another. It is like church. They are singing to the rhythm of the universe and I want to dance to their rhythm. They pause and I know that although I am blinded I am not blinded in my mind; I understand what is happening. I am not sure that blind is the correct word because that implies the absence of sight is the abnormal state, but I feel like I have always been this way. I am the leader, and they are really singing in response to my words. And although I can't understand the words I am singing, I know they are the correct ones. The snake smiles at me.

The crowd is singing to Marie, which I understand that I am her with all my heart and soul. The snake is wrapping himself around my outstretched arm, and I hear a bell. The bell continues and grows louder as it turns into a familiar telephone ring and I sense that I am being summoned. The crowd falls away, and I feel the familiar reversal of sleep beginning; I am sensing sunlight as I try to hold onto to remnants of my dream.

# 4

TO AMBER, IT REALLY DIDN'T MATTER how she had met David. They were workout partners. He gave Amber a reason to look forward to her workouts without worrying about the "daily torture" she chose to endure. Just getting a chance to look at David made it all worthwhile. She wasn't dead, after all, just married.

David was what Amber's friends back home would term "seriously sexy". Yup, he had "it", whatever that was. Physically, he looked like he might have been a Greek sculpture of a discus thrower or some other character from the mythology Amber liked to read as a child. He was perfect to Amber. David stood a little over six feet tall, just the right height. In her daydreams, (and sometimes night dreams), Amber would fit perfectly under his arm but not too tall that kissing him might be uncomfortable. She dated a guy once who was too tall and didn't like only being waist high to her man.

David also had the right kind of butt. Amber was definitely into butts. It wasn't too high, like a basketball-player butt, nor was it too round. Instead, it was just right; David's butt was sinewy, a cross between a runner-butt and a baseball player-butt. In addition to this fantastic physique, David's voice resonated with a killer baritone that made the pit of Amber's stomach rumble when he spoke. The tiny smile on his face when her talked to her made it obvious he knew it too. Sometimes, while they were working out, he would purposely sing under his breath, as if he could sense what it did to her. He would just start singing, but really only loud enough for the two of them to hear. He would laugh deep and low as he watched Amber struggling to keep her cool. He sounded so good to Amber; he gave both Barry White and Teddy Pendergrass a run for their money, at least in her book he did. David had what it took to make a sista's panties wet!

David and Amber met everyday at the local Gold's gym, usually first thing in the morning before work. It was obvious to everyone in the gym that Amber and David were attracted to each other, although they both thought that they were hiding their feelings. The wedding rings on their fingers also made it obvious that they were both married; albeit to other people. Although she was attracted to David, Amber was determined that nothing was going to happen between them as long as she was married to Tyler. Now it didn't look like they were going to be married long.

Amber thought about it while she did her 30-minute cardiovascular exercise on the Stairmaster. It wasn't that she and Tyler fought all the time or didn't love one another; it was just that nothing physical was happening between them. Her relationship with Tyler was stagnant. Amber loved him, but she wasn't *in love* with him; there was no affection, no nothing. And, the sex was bad. Amber wasn't sure the sex had ever been good for her. She didn't fault him entirely for this, she wasn't sure she had learned how to enjoy the sexual act itself yet. Thinking about it, she admitted to herself she was often more excited by her sexual fantasies than she was by her husband. Amber didn't know what to do; Tyler was her first. Although she felt young, the spark was gone from their relationship and their sex life. There were probably 90 year-olds experiencing more passion than Tyler and Amber were.

It wasn't always like this; Tyler used to be very romantic. Amber often thought back to high school, when as young lovers, she and Tyler snuck into the high school theater together after school. They were both in that year's musical production and knew the backstage area well, so they had decided to have a private backstage picnic together.

Reminiscing about that picnic now made the event seem kinda corny to Amber. Tyler was the male lead in the play while she was a chorus member. Tyler was so romantic, he made Amber feel as if she were his leading lady. He had thought out all the details, including bringing all kinds of picnic foods along with matching plates and napkins. He even brought Pink Champale. Everybody drank that stuff back then, but it still made Amber kind of woozy, and of course, everything required that they feed each other.

They sat together, on an old lawn chair, as they ate and sipped the Pink Champale in the darkened school building. The light from the single candle Tyler had provided cast shadows on the walls and ceiling that otherwise would have been menacing.

They were so busy hugging each other and their heads were so full of Pink Champale, they didn't even feel the lawn chair breaking until it hit the floor with a thud. Amber remembered comparing the shock of them hitting the floor to a telephone ringing directly in her ear, waking her up out of a deep sleep. But those romantic days were over.

Amber and Tyler had finally talked when she could get him away from the television, and instead of discussing her graduate school dreams like she thought they would, they ended up talking about the future of their relationship. He beat Amber to the punch.

"I don't know about you Amber, but I am just not happy."

"Really?" Amber was surprised. She had thought she would

have to pry it out of him.

The root of his unhappiness had nothing to do with Amber at all, and after 10 years of being with Tyler, Amber was beginning to recognize this, even if he wasn't. Tyler could not deal well with transitions, and he was again at a major transition point in his life.

"I'm not sure I love you anymore."

"Oh? Yeah, I know what you mean."

Amber might as well let him talk. She wasn't surprised that he would think it was her fault. They had gone through this once before, so Amber could see it coming. She seemed to be the only one experiencing deja-vu.

When they first moved to Texas, Tyler would sit on the sofa in his dingy underwear, like clockwork every Friday after work. He would grab the remote and sit in the same spot on the sofa, just like he was doing now, continuously flipping through the channels. He wouldn't really watch what whizzed by on the screens, but he wouldn't talk to Amber either. He didn't go out or talk to his friends or family. He wouldn't move, except to use the bathroom or to eat. He probably burned more calories moving his hand from his mouth to his plate than doing anything else.

Looking back, it was obvious to Amber why he was unhappy with his life, and whatever he was having a hard time dealing with was affecting everything around him.

Now, at a similar transition point in his life, Tyler was back to sitting on the sofa, but this time talk shows held his attention. They seemed to provide an escape from his problems. The problems of these other people on the talk shows were so much more interesting. If he were a client, Amber might have thought they helped him keep his life in perspective. His military career was about to be over because of his accidents. He was being forced to make a move to civilian life and would have to go out and actually look for jobs like everyone else. It seemed to be just too much for him.

Amber could not tell to what extent this made Tyler feel like a failure. In his mind, he was jobless! He was the man and was supposed to be the breadwinner in the family. It was in the Bible, for goodness sakes! Amber was making more than he was, and to Tyler, it looked like she was having a good time doing it.

To Tyler, it seemed like Amber didn't worry about anything. Rather than deal with all of this, Tyler withdrew into himself and was trying to be happy in his own, private way. He was trying to lose himself in his talk show world, where everyone seemed to have worse problems than his.

During their discussion, Amber tried to make it easy for him.

"Maybe we only get 10 years together," she said. Tyler didn't seem to react at first.

"That is actually a long time. We tried our best, didn't we? It's okay for it to be over." Tyler answering, seemingly trying to convince himself of this more than anything, his eye seemed to be focusing somewhere past where Amber was sitting. She looked at him, and realized that she had been telling herself the same thing for a while. She knew that one of the reasons they stayed together for so long was because they both really hated failing at anything. They always tried to be the best at everything, so failure was an unacceptable. Maybe he would begin to believe it was okay not to be perfect too.

In addition to the fear of failure issue, they both felt as if they fit each other like a pair of old, overused blue jeans. They were comfortable with each other. It wasn't exactly an ideal or glamorous situation, but their marriage was safe.

After Amber and Tyler were married about eighteen months, they separated. They had just moved to their home in Austin, and Tyler had recently returned from his month-long field duty in Germany. To occupy herself while he was away, Amber got two jobs. During the day, Amber worked for a brokerage firm, and at night, she was a cocktail waitress at a comedy club. She enjoyed both of her jobs. She hadn't really built up a clientele yet with the brokerage firm, but it allowed her to feel like she was using the degree she worked so hard to earn, even if she wasn't exactly working in her field. It also gave her an excuse to get dressed up. Sometimes it was hard to tell which one of these was her favorite part.

The comedy club, on the other hand, provided a lot of extra cash. Amber always gave the black patrons extra-nice service, so she often ended up with much bigger tips than the rest of the wait staff. On an average night, while the other waitresses made about 30 to 40 dollars, it wasn't unusual for Amber to make close to 90 bucks! In addition, the other club employees thought she was glamorous.

In the beginning, Amber really thought that Austin, Texas was Small-Town-USA, and the other employees didn't know quite what to make of her. She seemed different to them and their daily fussing over Amber became a ritual. Her co-workers often commented on how they loved her flowing, leonine hair and often commented on how she was able to style it in a multitude of ways.

Her almond-shaped, hazel green eyes complemented her face, making her look somewhat "exotic". Then, Black people with light features were always "exotic" to white people in the South. That was the P.C. thing to say. In their southern minds, Amber was somehow different than those Black people they were used to seeing if they were bold enough to cross over Interstate 35 and venture to the East Side, the Black side of town. Black Austin may as well have been as far away as China rather than the short 15 minutes it was!

Since she was working all of the time, Tyler thought she was gone entirely too much. He thought Amber must have been cheating on him; for him that was the only explanation. Seeing Amber enjoying her jobs made him insecure, and it didn't help that she was making as much if not more than he was, even if it took her two jobs to do it. He was so busy sitting on the sofa flipping channels, their sex life was almost non-existent. Tyler couldn't understand this part; Amber acted like she was too good to do it on the sofa. Hell, when they were in high school, at their stage picnic, they made out on a lawn chair, so why couldn't she get busy on the sofa? Tyler thought he knew what to do, just like his pops always did when he was little. He was going to show Amber a thing or two about who wore the pants in the family.

One Friday evening, as Amber walked through door she came face-to-face with a double-barreled shotgun pointed at her temple. Before she could even get out her usual "Hi, Honey" she was cut short.

"Where the fuck have you been!"

Tyler was in a complete rage. Amber felt time slowing down as she realized Tyler was sitting there with his shotgun, waiting for her to come through the door. She looked down and saw piles of clothes, her clothes, strewn about the floor. It looked as if Tyler was trying to help her pack her things. Amber lifted her gaze from the floor to Tyler, noticing the challenge in his eyes and his temples as they pulsated with anger. Obviously, Tyler had decided he had enough of whatever he thought was going on. Amber didn't know what that was and didn't wait to ask.

Amber was from an entirely different type of family than Tyler, and she couldn't imagine two adults hurting each other. The only marriages she ever saw seemed to be perfect; things like this just didn't happen! Before she knew it, she slapped the barrel of the shotgun out of her face, and only knew what happened next because Tyler later described it to her.

Tyler never fired the gun, and Amber ended with a few bruises on her face to show for the whole incident. She would remember later that the bruises came when Tyler pinned her face to the stucco-covered wall to keep her from hurting herself or him. She used every part of her body, as well as any object within her reach to try and pummel his 280-lb. body until she felt the coarse surface of the stucco against her face.

Without thinking, she grabbed the closest thing to her and flung it up against the side of her husband's head. Tyler let out a piercing yell as the hot iron hit the side of his face. As usual, Amber had left it plugged in after she ironed her clothes before work.

When the iron made contact with Tyler's head, his yell echoed as Amber watched his blood suddenly appear on her white rug. Although she had the rug professionally cleaned later, Amber always saw the ghost of that bloodstain clearly, haunting her. Tyler carried both internal and external scars resulting from that incident for a long, long time. They were there as a reminder anytime he thought of resorting to violence with Amber.

Amber told her father about the whole thing. She had to convince her close-knit family not to travel from Louisiana to Austin to kill Tyler or not to put any "voodoo spells" on him, but Amber and Tyler decided to split up. She actually filed for divorce, and then decided not to go to court. It was easier for them to get back together and take all the comments from their families than it was for them to admit to failing at their marriage.

Glancing down at the display on her exercise machine, Amber stopped reviewing her relationship with Tyler, and she couldn't believe the stupid choices she made. Here she was, at the gym, with incredibly sexy David, sweating her butt off while her ex-football-playing-now-fat husband slept at home. Sexy David was also married, with a small son who was his spitting image, and he was her neighbor from across the street.

They had become quite good friends over the past few months, but they had not been intimate with each other, at least not yet. That did not mean Amber hadn't imagined being held in David's sexy arms. She actually played the scene over and over in her mind, and several times, her body was racked by orgasm at the mere thought of David's caress.

They started to meet outside the health club just last week. He would leave work early and just happen to be at the library, every day, on campus, where Amber went to study. The first time he showed up on campus, Amber was surprised. Soon enough, the library became one of their favorite places. They talked and laughed and got to know each other better there without other people watching.

The library was just one of the places Amber frequented that David appeared. Another was the local club. There were a lot of clubs in Austin, but there was only one that had a steady Black clientele. Most of them did not feature music that appealed to a Black crowd on a regular basis.

Thursday nights were girls' nights out, and Amber often went out with her friends. The local club played R & B on Thursdays to try to attract Black clientele, and this was one of Amber's crowds' favorite places. Amber soon noticed that David was often there too. He rarely said more than hello, and only once did he actually dance with her. Other times he just seemed to watch from the distance. Amber speculated that he left his wife at home; he always seemed to be there alone.

David knew Tyler was often out of town. He suggested that perhaps, just maybe, one of those times, he and Amber might get together for dinner. Amber was reluctant. If they met at night that would technically be classified as a date. A date meant she would be officially cheating on her husband. And for all her good Catholic upbringing, that would be a sin. Although she had long since switched religions, the idea of a date with someone other than Tyler was unacceptable. Besides, the Black community in Austin was tiny; she might run into someone she knew. It was one thing being together in daylight, but after dark there were no excuses that Amber could use to explain her way out of that situation. It would still look like something was going on, even if nothing was. That would still be considered sinful.

Tyler was twice Amber's weight, so it wasn't a good idea to have him throwing that weight around because of a careless grapevine rumor! She could hear the vultures talking now, "Girl, did you see Amber and David? I wonder what that's about?"

The truth of the matter was Amber and David were friends, and he was telling her things she needed to hear at the time, such as how beautiful he thought she was. He gave her the romance she missed and needed. Although Amber did not admit it yet, their relationship was already a romance.

"I don't understand what Tyler is thinking, letting you slip away like this. He better wake up and smell the coffee before I do".

Sometimes David was so self-confident; he bordered on self-possession. He was fast getting to the point where he wasn't even trying to conceal his rap.

Like many of her friends, Amber was a romantic. David knew what to do and how to do it. He knew exactly what to suggest to make her sentimental and mushy. He often said things that left Amber thinking he was such a sensitive guy, and she was a sucker for sensitivity.

In addition to her other jobs, Amber was always involved in one plan or another to make extra money. One of them was a multi-level marketing plan that involved selling health food products. David was not really interested, but he must have purchased a year's worth of bee pollen. He had used the pollen purchase as an excuse to introduce himself to Amber. Actually, he had introduced himself to both her and Tyler, and then afterwards spent hours in their living room talking with Tyler.

Tyler didn't know David was the kind of man husbands fear. Actually, maybe he could tell because he commented on several occasions that he felt David was not to be trusted. When Amber questioned him, he refused to provide any details. Maybe Tyler could see David had no scruples. He didn't care if someone was married or not, even to his best friend, and Tyler was just an acquaintance. As long as a person had something he wanted or could give him something he needed, he would try and get over. He really believed all was fair in love and war, and he lived by no one's honor code but his own.

David was the kind of guy that when he got married the single guys cheered. In addition to being smooth, he was very good looking. He had apple-pie charm in a strange kind of way; not as wholesome as you might first think. He was fair-skinned with almond-shaped, emerald green eyes, not un-like Amber's, that could be seductive in an instant, and he stood about six feet two inches. David's hair was light brown and curly, and he had freckles, with a crooked, Howdy Doody kind of smile. He was what Amber's father called "one of those beige people". He acted as if his statements didn't apply to Amber. "You can never really be sure about them folk," her father would say. In many ways, it was not really possible to tell what race David was. He was either a very light-skinned Black man, or darker complected white guy, but it didn't matter. David was what Amber needed him to be. The thought never crossed her mind that he might not be Black. Although she was from a multiracial family herself, the possibility of her dating outside her race, which she considered to be Black, was not acceptable.

When Amber was getting close to dating age, she was told, in a not-so-round about way, that she could do whatever she wanted away from home, but bringing a white man home to her all-Black neighborhood was out of the question. Her father thought life would be complicated enough for Amber without her complicating it further. This was a constant source of amusement for Amber throughout her dating years. She reminded her father of her mother's tallow-hued complexion that was often mistaken for white.

"Octoroon don't qualify as white!" he would say. "One drop is all it takes!" He was so old-fashioned that it made Amber's skin crawl. The first time her father made that comment, Amber had to look up what octoroon meant.

Although David loved to tell Amber his story of being pulled over by state troopers and passing for White to avoid a ticket, when he was around Amber, he acted Black. Or at least he did in her mind.

That's what made Amber and David different. In actuality, David and Amber were nearly the same complexion, but unlike David, Amber felt no need to walk on the other side. She always was secure with her ethnic identity.

Although the majority of her mother's family was white, Amber was raised by her father's family; Black people. In fact, it was almost the only family she knew. To deny being Black would be to disrespect her family and her ancestors, and Amber could never do that. Although she didn't always agree with her family and was sometimes embarrassed by the things they did and believed, Amber could not bring herself to deny who she was even if she didn't exactly broadcast her family tree to the world.

David claimed he didn't know who his biological parents were, and that a couple from England had adopted him. His adoptive mother was biracial, and his adoptive father was white. Supposedly, they were rich shipbuilders who now lived in southern Florida. Amber could never verify this story because they never seemed to visit, and David claimed not to have any pictures of them.

When they wanted to see David, he just disappeared, and he was very good at disappearing. Sometimes he would go away for days, claiming to have been to see his folks via the family business' corporate jet. When his parents missed him, he said, they would send the "plane" out to Austin to pick him up. His whole world was Fantasy Island!

Often, the places David disappeared to were virtually unverifiable. He was so slick and changed his story so often, it was impossible to tell where his life stopped and imagination began. Amber didn't pursue the race issue with David, it really didn't matter to her. For her, Black was not really a color, but a state of mind, and even though he had "Vanilla Ice " looks, everything else about him, from his sure-footed stride to the meticulous way he dressed, made him Soul Brother Number One in her book.

After that initial meeting with Amber and Tyler, David watched and waited. Whenever Amber came outside her house, so did he. He would pretend to sweep his porch until she left. Sometimes, after dark, he would act as if he were sweeping his porch so he could look through her lit windows, hoping he would see her.

They originally became workout partners because he watched her so much that he knew her schedule. He knew when she went to Gold's gym. One day he just showed up too, "accidentally on purpose".

"I didn't know you worked out here!" He said while flashing his best smile at Amber. He was so enthusiastic he even made Amber glad to see herself.

"We must be on the same schedule or something, David".

"We must be. I am here a little early today, though." Amber had no idea David planned his visits to the gym so that they would coincide with hers.

Amber had tried to convince Tyler to go to the gym with her for some time. Since his accident, he seemed to have lost interest in his appearance and was eating himself into oblivion. Tyler put on the pounds, making it easy for David to work his way into Amber's good graces. Amber was ready to have a workout partner and David's timing was great. He was fit, he was enthusiastic, and he was interested in Amber.

# 5

CHE HAD BALLS and Amber liked her because of it. Che was the pastor's daughter at the church Tyler and Amber joined in Austin. She had made Amber feel welcome and at home. It was also the first church Amber joined as an adult.

Before meeting Che, Amber had not attended church as a member in a long while. Although she had stopped being Catholic after she was confirmed, Amber had become really disillusioned with the Catholic faith when her favorite cousin was killed by a stray bullet back in New Orleans. John and Amber were around the same age and spent a lot of time together while they were growing up.

John was on his way to the neighborhood grocery store when out of nowhere, a bullet came through the store window he was standing in front of and pierced his skull. Amber saw it happen; John was on his way to the store to meet her. Amber was upset for a long time; she and John had a lot in common. They were very close, and he had big dreams of leaving New Orleans and exploring life just like Amber had.

He never knew what hit him. After he was shot, he turned and kept right on walking down the street and talking to his friend, never missing a beat in his sentence. Amber watched as the bullet appeared to come right out the other side of his head, slightly above his temple.

By the time John fell, Amber had finally reached him. She sat on the ground next to him and put his bloody head in her lap, telling him it was going to be alright. As she did, she replayed the whole incident over and over in her mind; it kept happening in slow motion. Later she would compare the hole the bullet had left in the window to the almost identical one she remembered in her cousin's head, thinking that if other people hadn't noticed John was shot, perhaps he wouldn't have noticed either. Maybe, he would have continued walking, right up to Amber, hugged her like he always did, and things would have been okay.

When the paramedics took her cousin away, the first thing Amber did was to go to St. Anne's Catholic Church. It was right on the corner, near the place where her cousin's shooting had occurred. Struggling to remember what to do, she lit a candle and prayed to God to make her cousin all right. She asked God to punish the person who pulled the trigger. John died anyway, and although everyone in the neighborhood knew who the shooter was, he was never arrested. This type of thing was an all too common occurrence in the 'hood. Amber's prayers were not answered, and she felt betrayed. At that point, she decided the Catholic god was not for her.

Amber's quest for religion never really stopped over the years. She always felt as if something were missing. Much to the dismay of her family, she stopped going to Catholic Church and began to visit other churches with friends.

She went to Kingdom Hall with friends who were Jehovah's Witnesses. She liked that there were no collections and that the meetings were conducted like one great big lecture. She watched as the men in the congregation practiced witnessing to a group of listeners and she watched as the women in the congregation did the same thing, but to other women and children. Amber was impressed as some of the men would stand at the podium and give speeches with authority, reminding Amber of video clips she had seen of Martin Luther King, Jr. and Malcolm X speaking to groups during the civil rights movement.

Amber wanted to give speeches like she saw the men do, but she was told she couldn't. The elders in the congregation told her men were called to give speeches, not women. This was enough for Amber to move on; she decided that Jehovah was obviously sexist, and Kingdom Hall was not for her.

From that point, Amber stayed away from houses of worship for awhile. It wasn't a conscious thing; it was the practice of religion just did not appeal to her much. She still believed in the existence of a greater being, but she just wasn't sure how this being should be worshipped.

Right before they got married, Amber did go to church with Tyler. His family was Pentecostal, and they were invited to a special service at his uncle's church. Amber had avoided going to church with him during the whole time they were dating. The whole Pentecostal faith was a mystery to her. In Catholicism, the priests generally did not own the church. The idea that Tyler's uncle was the Pastor and owner of this church was a little strange to Amber.

For the most part, the service scared Amber. The music was a lot louder and the congregation more verbal than she was used to. In general, during a Catholic service, the congregation did not speak unless they were spoken to or praying in unison. In this Pentecostal service, people yelled out whenever they wanted to.

The service was frequently punctuated by "Ar'ight, now!" and "Well!" At one point, the pastor invited people up to the altar for prayer. Tyler all but dragged her up there, with a Cheshire cat grin on his face the entire way. Getting to the altar seemed more like a sojourn than the few steps that it actually was. Amber's face was beet-red from embarrassment as the short distance seemed to stretch into a mile like in a scene from Alice in Wonderland. With every step, Amber became more and more conscious of the sweat that was coming through her dress.

Once they got to the altar, Tyler's uncle anointed her forehead with oil and started to pray, asking the Lord to cast the demons out of her. At the same time, a woman who was standing next to Amber started to babble incoherently. Tyler told her later the woman was talking in tongues.

Amber had never seen anything like it. At most of the other churches she attended, the services were much more reserved. It was too much for her. She wasn't aware she had been possessed by demons; she was very confused. In addition, the people were doing what looked like yelling and screaming and dancing to Amber. The only other times she had seen anything like it was on television.

Amber was scared, but she was also too embarrassed to leave. Everyone else in the small church seemed to be just fine with all the goings on. Amber just stood her ground and hoped the whole thing would be over soon.

In all, the church service lasted well over three hours. By the time the service was over, her butt ached from sitting. This was of far cry from the half-hour services she experienced growing up. Later Tyler would laugh at her.

"At least our services have some soul! In Catholic Church, I feel like it is over as soon as you say Praise the Lord, Amen!"

When she finally got out of there, Amber was done with church for good. It would be several years before she visited a church again. And although Tyler made fun of her, he wasn't rushing to church either. He talked brimstone and hellfire, but all he really wanted to do was sleep on Sunday mornings. When they moved to Austin, a couple who befriended Amber and Tyler invited them to visit their church, and so as not to insult the couple, they agreed to go. The couple attended a United Methodist Church in East Austin. To her surprise, Amber really enjoyed the service. It seemed to fall somewhere between Catholicism and Tyler's Pentecostal church. One thing that really impressed Amber was instead of focusing on the suffering, this new church seemed to focus on the happiness in religion. Everybody seemed to be happy, especially Che.

Che sat behind her in church that first day. After the service, she promptly introduced herself, that is, right after she introduced herself to Tyler. She stuck her hand right in between them, all the time cheesing at Tyler.

"Hi, I'm Che. And you would be?"

"Tyler Montpelier. This is my wife Amber LaReaux. Nice to meet you."

Tyler was caught a little off guard by Che's forwardness. Che now turned to Amber, letting her eyes check out Amber from head to toe.

"Well, ain't you lucky?" She said.

Her crooked smiled hinted of her perfectly white, perfectly straight teeth behind her lips. Amber felt herself standing up taller as she extended her hand toward Che's. She raised an eyebrow but didn't answer. Che continued.

"Welcome to our church."

Amber and Che shook hands and exchanged numbers. Although Che seemed to be checking out her husband, Amber liked her.

Amber and Che were literally as different as night and day. Whenever they were together, people would whisper about the contrast between swarthy complected Che and Amber's light, freckled skin. Amber's tall, slim figure seemed to be in direct contrast to Che's compactness. But their physical differences didn't stop their friendship.

Over time, their friendship seemed to hover somewhere between love and hate. Amber admired and envied Che and her free-spirited nature. In that respect, Che was everything Amber did not have the guts to be.

Che was a freak! Right at the start of their friendship, Che shared her motto with Amber.

"Friends are friends for life, but men, Tchh! They are expendable".

She said it in a matter-of-fact kind of way, like it was gospel. She didn't even blink. Amber gasped.

"You are horrible, girl! People shouldn't be thrown away." Amber could not hold back her smile. Che really believed that, she could tell.

Che was strong in ways Amber could never hope to be. Che was even uninhibited sexually and was not afraid to admit it.

Amber knew because Che would always tell her. Amber

would act as if she were appalled at the way Che behaved and she would remind Che to use condoms, but she would often wish that she enjoyed sex as much as Che did.

Amber also liked the way Che never fussed over her appearance. She never wore much makeup and her skin always looked fantastic. Amber's skin was flawless too, but it was flawless because she applied her makeup meticulously, the way she had been taught in the Che-proclaimed "ghetto-bourgeoisie" finishing school her father had insisted she attend. Che always found great natural styles for her hair. Because she never worked hard at letting her natural beauty shine through, Amber admired her.

Che loved and hated Amber too. She really admired the way Amber appeared to be so self-confident and seemed to have her life mapped out. Che never knew what she wanted to do with her life past five o'clock in the afternoon, much less in terms of a career. What she didn't know was Amber always appeared so cool because she had become really good at masking her insecurities. So good in fact, she seemed to mask them from herself. But in many ways, Che was jealous of Amber's life. She appeared to know where she was going, and everything she did seemed to have a certain flavor to it that attracted other people like flies to honey. Men seemed to like her and not because she had a reputation for being very good at certain sexual acts, either. They liked talking to Amber and fussed over her features and clothing. Che agreed with them on this; she thought Amber looked great in everything!

What Che didn't realize was that more than anything, she

herself was the reason more men were attracted to Amber. It had nothing to do with Amber at all. Outside of church, Che always seemed to be angry at the world, and whenever the two of them would go out, she made no attempt to hide this anger. Anyone who came near her wanted to be somewhere else. Amber, on the other hand, was always smiling, and people liked this, even if her smiles were hiding how she really felt inside.

One Thursday night, for instance, Amber and Che went to the club, for R&B night as usual. As soon as they walked in, one of the regulars asked Amber for a dance. She smiled and waved over her shoulder to Che, immediately heading for the small dusty dance floor. She loved to dance and usually she would spend most of the night there. Amber glanced back at Che. She noticed Che had taken a seat at a table near the place the two of them had been standing. She could see that Che was pouting and sullen.

Che stayed at that table all-night and turned down everyone who asked her to dance. Her favorite drink was a blue kool aide, and she sat there drinking big blue drink after big blue drink. Even though Amber was her friend and was obviously having a good time, her shifting in her seat and the black look that stayed on her face made it obvious to Amber she was getting madder and madder. She ordered drink after drink; her drunkenness would give her the excuse she needed to be nasty to Amber.

All through the night, other people in the club kept asking Amber about Che. "What's up with your friend?" they wanted to know. Amber just shrugged her shoulders. She really didn't even want to deal with Che's unpleasantness that night. Whatever the problem, it was Che's to deal with, not hers.

Amber watched Che but refused to feel sorry for her. She knew Che was jealous, but she didn't care. In fact, she enjoyed it. Girls' night out was her one night to be free of Tyler and his morbid attitude, and she wasn't about to let some sourpuss spoil it. Amber used every opportunity she could to rub it in. Whenever she thought Che was watching, Amber laughed louder and tried to appear more dynamic. Basically, she put on the best "bitch" act she could.

As the night wore on, Che finally drank herself into a blue haze and now no one dared approach her. It was as if her foul attitude had enveloped her, creating an impenetrable wall that no one could or would even attempt to break through. As Amber was talking with some of the other regulars, Che finally unglued her ass from her seat and walked over. Amber drew in her breath as she watched her approach.

" I'm ready to go now, Amber," Che said with an angry look on her face. Her full lips were pressed into a straight line. Amber looked at her in mock surprise; they usually stayed until closing.

"Really?" she said coyly. " I'm not, but I will be in about half an hour. That okay?"

She threw a wan smile in Che's direction and walked away before she could answer. She knew it wasn't okay.

Che just wanted to leave; she wasn't having a good time and

she needed to go to the bathroom. It was obvious from the tense, cartoon-like straight line her lips formed that she was fuming! There was no mistaking that she was ready! She caught up to Amber and looked her squarely in the eye.

"Is your husband waiting up for you tonight?"

She gave her back the same coy smile that Amber had given her. She waited for her response.

Amber didn't respond. Instead she turned and acted as if she were looking around for someone to dance with. The cloudy look returned to Che's face. She grabbed Amber's arm, spinning her back around to face her.

"Look," she said, "You can stay if you want to, but I'm going home. You bitches are the only ones who are having fun anyway. Besides, nobody wants to talk to or dance with me. These assholes as so superficial, they are only interested in light skinned hoes with green eyes, straight hair and big butts." Che turned and stormed away.

Everyone was stunned. Amber was speechless; Che's words stung her face as if she were slapped with a wet, open-palm. The music boomed in the background and the corridor of silence that stretched between the two friends was the loudest thing in the room. Everyone in the little group watched Che walk away. In ten minutes, she had picked up some guy who she obviously planned to substitute for Amber's ride home. Amber watched her from across the dance floor and just let her go. She was so angry with Che for embarrassing herself with her outburst that she didn't care whether Che got home okay or not. She deserved whatever she got!

Amber forgave Che, or at least she swept the incident under the carpet, but she didn't forget it. Their conversation the next day was stilted, like each was waiting for the other to bring it up.

"Hello…" Amber knew Che was on the phone before she even picked it up.

"Hey, girl, what's up? Feel like the mall?"

Che's voice lacked its usual enthusiasm for their weekend mall runs; she knew Amber was angry with her. Amber could tell that Che she really didn't remember what happened, courtesy of too many blue kool aides, but it was obvious she knew she had fucked up. Che did make a mental note not to drink so much. Hopefully that would help to keep some of her nastier thoughts under control. They plodded through the rest of the conversation.

"Sure, I will meet you in front of Dillard's."

Neither Amber nor Che mentioned the prior night's incident. They acted like it was a hiccup in their relationship. By the time they met at the mall, it was as if nothing happened at all.

# 6

ALTHOUGH AMBER AND CHE WERE FRIENDS, Amber never mentioned the problems she and Tyler were having. She didn't share any information about her relationship with David either. She kept her silence for quite a long while, until right before she went back home to Louisiana with Tyler for Christmas. She decided to visit Che before she left and was so upset she couldn't hide her feelings anymore. Che's hello barely made it past her lips before Amber burst into tears.

"I am so unhappy." Amber was sobbing like a two-year-old. "I don't know what to do. Tyler doesn't love me, I can tell." She hadn't honestly shared her feelings with anyone and as soon as the words were out of her mouth, she felt better. She shared all of the details with Che- almost. She told her why she thought Tyler was unhappy, and she told her about her friendship with David, leaving out the parts about how attracted she was to him.

Che was not surprised about Amber's feelings about her relationship with Tyler. To her, it was obvious something was going on between them. Amber and Tyler never went anywhere together. Recently Tyler called Che several times; in a round about way, he was double-checking on Amber's whereabouts. He made one of those calls just yesterday, and Che didn't pass up the opportunity to tease him.

"Excuse you," she said, "But are you trying to find out where Amber is? Why don't you just come out and ask me?!"

"C'mon Che! Well, do you know where she is?"

"Ain't she your wife?"

Tyler paused. "Damn! I should apologize..."

"No, don't apologize Tyler. She ain't here. But your insecurities are showing! I am sure she will turn up! Or should I call the hospitals?" Che could not resist the chance to be a little facetious. Tyler sucked his teeth and hung up.

The idea that Amber and David forged a friendship *was* a surprise to Che. Amber never mentioned anything at all about it. She kept her business with David a little too secret. But Che couldn't blame Amber; David was definitely fine!

She saw him once when she visited Amber; he came across the street to talk with them. At the time, Che recalled checking him out from head to toe, noting the outline his bulge made in his jogging shorts that were just a little too tight. Che wasn't even embarrassed when she dropped the broom she was holding and it hit David in the groin. "Oh," she tee-heed, "I am sooo sorry!"

She kept her gaze glued to his shorts as if she were mesmerized. "I hope I didn't hurt the family jewels too badly!"

Amber, on the other hand, was so embarrassed that if she could have picked up the pavement and pulled it over her head, she would have. Che finally unglued her eyes from David's shorts and looked up; she flashed her best smile as she batted her eyelashes. It was as if someone pushed her "flirt" button. She may not have been the best at a lot of things, but she sure was good at flirting.

Amber's sobbing pushed Che's vision of David from her mind, and she stepped aside so her friend could come inside her apartment. She wouldn't take this opportunity to rib Amber about her prior silence about all of this stuff. She sensed Amber needed comforting and just listened.

They sat on the floor in Che's apartment, and Che hugged Amber as she cried, supplying the tissues when necessary. As she listened, Che felt herself tuning Amber's words out and concentrating on the way she sucked her breath in before she began each phrase. She noticed how Amber's long, slender fingers twirled the tissues she was handed until they fell apart.

Just as Amber had not shared her feelings with Che, she had not shared a part of herself with Amber. She knew Amber felt she was a little wild sexually and she thought if she were completely honest with Amber, she might terminate their friendship.

Amber was so busy crying she didn't notice the strange look on Che's face. Being aware of the feelings of the people around her was never one of Amber's strong points, especially when she was supposed to be the center of attention. Amber didn't even notice as Che moved closer to her and began stroking her hair. Before either of them realized what was happening, Che was kissing Amber. It started as a brush on the cheek in a comforting way, but Che was *really* kissing Amber; not like a friend comforting a distressed friend, but more like a man kissing a woman!

Amber stood up so fast she almost lost her balance. She was shocked; the whole thing was just too much for her to handle, especially now. She found she had difficulty speaking.

"I gotta go," she stammered. She headed for the door, trying to get as far away from Che as possible.

Che was speechless; she could barely get out an apology.

"Wait, I'm sorr—"

"We'll talk later." Amber's breath was quick and short. At this point, she was out the door, halfway to her car.

Che knew from Amber's reaction that she had made a mistake. She knew it would be a mistake before she began; she had imagined herself with Amber on more than one occasion and it always ended just the way it did then. In fact, Che had been attracted to Amber for long time. She knew Amber was too uptight to even consider having anything other than a platonic relationship with her.

Amber and Che often joked about Amber's Catholic guilt, so Che knew Amber would never consider having a sexual relationship with another woman. Amber would say that it would be okay for Che to have bisexual feelings, but not okay for her to act on them. She just hoped that what she had done did not ruin their friendship for good.

As Amber got into her car, she fumbled with her keys trying to get them into the ignition. She found herself unable to hold onto any single key; it took three tries before she got the correct one in and turned it. She pulled away from Che's house very fast, her mind whirling, almost completely forgetting she was upset about her problems with Tyler. As she drove home, she kept thinking about Che making a pass at her. Amber felt so naive! How could she not see that Che was bisexual! But then again, she never seemed to be able to sense these things. It's not like this was the first time something like this happened to her. What was it about her that other women found sexually attractive? What she giving off the wrong signals? Maybe she walked different or something.

The first time Amber had contact with a lesbian was while she was in college. In the summer of her junior year, she wanted some excitement in her life, so she took a job in a jewelry showroom owned by a friend's father in New York. She'd met a lot of interesting people that summer. One of them was the security guard who happened to be a lesbian.

When they first told her Danielle was a lesbian, Amber was really uncomfortable. She didn't know how to act, so she just ignored it. Soon it became a non-issue and she forgot about it. It just wasn't a big deal anymore.

Eventually Danielle and Amber became friends. Danielle confided in Amber. She was in a shaky relationship with her live-in girlfriend, and everyday she would update Amber on the latest developments in their rocky relationship.

Amber became her sounding board and would often dispense free advice to Danielle about what she thought was the appropriate thing to do about whatever predicament Danielle and her girlfriend were in at the time.

Just when Amber was feeling comfortable, Danielle made a pass at her. And just like with Che, Amber never even saw it coming. It happened right before closing time. All of the employees were straightening up. Amber was working behind her counter when Danielle approached her.

"Hey, woman!" Danielle greeted her. "What'cha doing later?" She didn't wait for her to answer. "How 'bout we go out and get us a drink?"

Amber thought about it for a minute and might have considered going; she didn't have any real plans. As they stood there, Danielle began smoothing Amber's blouse, making Amber so uncomfortable, she automatically stepped back. There was something about the way Danielle's hand slid over her blouse that let Amber know she wasn't being asked to have an ordinary drink with an ordinary girlfriend.

Before she could answer, Danielle added to the proposition.

"We could talk more, and you could tell me why you like men, and then I could show you why I like women." She arched one eyebrow as she paused, waiting for Amber's answer.

Her voice was deep and breathy, and she spoke in a manner that left no doubt in Amber's mind what Danielle intended. Amber watched, mouth opened with surprise as Danielle continued.

"Maybe you'll begin to see my point of view?"

Amber had drawn in her breath sharply. She began to understand the homophobia some men had, as if they were threatened by the mere presence of a gay man.

"Wait..." Amber stammered. She felt her palms beginning to sweat and noticed she was nervously twisting a pair of earrings she held in her hands.

"Aren't you a little bit curious?" Danielle leaned closer to Amber, forcing her to step back again although a counter was still between them. " I can take you places no man ever will, you know."

Amber watched Danielle smiling at her but hadn't known whether she should be flattered, insulted or angry. Although she had grown to like Danielle, her folks back home would say her New York friend was a freak and probably label her one too for even associating with Danielle. Amber didn't want to cause a scene. She looked around nervously, knowing that the others in the shop would love to get into her business. Although no one could see them, she felt that if she yelled or spoke too loudly, the grapevine would be buzzing with all sorts of rumors, probably eventually saying she and Danielle had a lovers' quarrel. That would be the last thing she needed; she still had four weeks left of the summer!

"Look, we can be friends but that is it!" Amber's voice was low and hissing. "If you want to continue this friendship, you better keep your shit on that side of the counter, and I will keep mine on this side! As long as you respect that, there will be no problems! Got it?!" It took everything she had to keep her voice down.

Now it was Danielle's turn to be surprised. She stepped back as if Amber's words shoved her back into her own personal space.

"I thought you were cool with this! Okay, I get it; I'll never mention it again. I didn't think you would get so upset!"

Her voice had changed from throaty to whimpering, almost like a child who was just slapped on the back of her hand.

Danielle stopped sharing her problems with Amber. In fact, she never really said much to Amber again. But Amber knew from the other employees that Danielle called her a tease and her feelings were hurt. From then on, Amber tried to be a little more alert about relationships with the other woman in the shop and in New York in general.

When she went back to school in the fall, she noticed there were definitely people who were gay or lesbian on her campus. It wasn't that they were new, she just hadn't noticed before. In fact, she noticed there was such a large contingent on campus that there was even a private lounge designated for them. Rumor had it the that lounge, sponsored by the Gay and Lesbian Society, was much more luxurious than those for other clubs. That fall Amber had her second encounter with another lesbian.

One of the campus celebrities was a sophomore named Toni Marshall. The summer before, she had become a one-hit-wonder when she released a semi-hip-hop/rap song that had gone platinum. Everyone on the yard knew who she was, but Amber had yet to meet her.

They met one day at the homecoming game, and to Amber's surprise, Toni was very nice. They ended up exchanging phone numbers. Before long, Toni was calling Amber on a regular basis. Eventually, she admitted to Amber she once had a female lover who was three years younger. When Toni's lover's parents discovered the nature of her relationship with Toni, the girl, who was still in high school at the time, was sent to live with her relatives in the Virgin Islands.

Toni had met Amber's brother and claimed to have a crush on him. She called Amber, and after they talked for awhile, she would always ask to speak to her brother. This went on for a stretch, until one day, Amber was in the lounge at school and she heard two guys talking.

Toni walked by but they couldn't see Amber sitting behind them. "There goes Toni, man. Check her out!"

"Yeah, she's fine, but you do know she is a little freaky-deaky."

"Yeah?! What do you mean? A little freak is okay with me!"

Amber could see him move his hand in that familiar side-to-side rocking motion as he spoke. Amber, eavesdropping, was not prepared for the next comment.

"Yah, man. She even told me she is doing both Amber AND her brother."

Amber was shocked. Just what was Toni "doing"? Doing what? She couldn't believe what she was hearing, but she knew what they meant. She picked up her things and scuttled away, hoping they had not realized she overheard them. As soon as she got to a phone, she immediately called her brother and told him what she overheard. He wasn't as shocked as Amber was, but he told Amber he would end his relationship with Toni. Amber stopped answering her phone for awhile, and just for good measure, she made sure that if she were seen with anyone repeatedly at school, that person was male.

Amber pulled her car into her parking spot at her Lake Hills apartment, realizing she didn't remember anything about driving the short distance from East Austin. She resigned that she would have to deal with Che later, but knew it would take awhile for her to be able to talk about it. She hated confrontations! She wished she could stop being so uncomfortable about her sexuality; she talked with folks all day about their problems but knew she had her own issues too. More than anything, she was shocked. Besides, there were more important things on her mind. She turned off her car, placing her Club on her steering wheel like always. As she started toward her door, the only thing on her mind was getting some sleep. Thank goodness Tyler was in his own world. She was exhausted.

# 7

IN HER MIND, things had changed. She no longer felt she had failed although she and Tyler were obviously going to break up. Tyler was the one who brought up being unhappy anyway, so it was really he who was calling it quits. He was giving up, not her. In her mind, that made it all right.

And of course Tyler would have this happen right before they visited Louisiana for Christmas. Tyler had found a new job, and after the holidays, he would be moving on. Amber was to stay behind in Austin to finish her master's degree, and follow him, again. At least that was the plan. They both agreed not to discuss the fate of their relationship until after Christmas.

Christmas day was a special time for them. It was the anniversary of Tyler and Amber's first official date, when they were still in high school. At the time, Amber was dating another guy, a college freshman. Before college, Kevin had attended high school with Amber and Tyler. He sat behind her in homeroom. There were no major sparks or whistles for her with Kevin; he was a summer romance.

As the weather cooled down and the holiday season approached, Amber's summer romance was cooling too. She began thinking about kicking her summer fling to the curb. Then, school started and life became more complicated than it was in the summer, and Kevin was taking up too much space. Her father didn't like him anyway. Kevin's mother took every opportunity to hit on her dad on more than one occasion, sometimes even with Amber's mother in the next room.

Her father was often quite comical about people he didn't like, especially if he felt they were not right for Amber. He made jokes about guys she brought home, and often his jokes would turn serious. For whatever reason, her dad really disliked Kevin. He took one look at him the first time they met and dubbed him "Old Anus Lips." No matter how often Amber reminded her father of the guy's name, he was forever referring to him by his new nickname. Amber was embarrassed to no end, but she knew she couldn't do anything about it. The name-calling would continue until the relationship ended.

On Christmas day, Amber was supposed to meet Kevin to

exchange gifts, but she stood him up. Tyler had put an end to those plans. Their imaginary stock had done well, and they had gotten an A in the class. Tyler decided to turn on the charm. He had showed up at Amber's place unexpectedly; dressed to the nines. He had decided to profess his undying deep "like". He looked great to Amber, especially when he was dressed up. He was in great shape, at least better than most of the other high school punks Amber knew, and definitely better than Kevin, who could, at best, be described as scrawny.

Tyler's football player's physique was at its best; his chiseled shoulders and chest showed through even the baggiest of clothes. No one wanted to be on his bad side. With him around, Amber felt protected. Tyler had a mustache, which made him look much older, a definite plus at 17. But the icing on the cake was that unlike most of the other boys she knew, Tyler had transportation. There was nothing like unlimited access to a car. As soon as her father let her date occasionally, Amber decided she was definitely not the take-the-bus-type, so Tyler's car helped his case with Amber quite a bit.

Amber was a sucker for romance, and Tyler had showed up prepared to pour it on. Amber remembered him, standing there.

"Hey."

"Hey, Amber."

"Don't you look nice?!"

"Isn't red your favorite color?"

Amber swept her eyes over his dark suit, immediately noticed his red shirt and red matching shoes.

"Yeah, yeah, it is." Amber could smell the musk of his cologne and was already imagining her nose buried in his neck.

"Aren't you going to ask me in, Amber?"

"Oh, I'm sorry." Amber stepped back from the door as she spoke. The smell of Tyler's cologne was heavy on her mind.

"What's that?" Tyler was carrying a teddy bear, half -wrapped in a hatbox. He had cut a whole in the hat box so that the bear's head could stick through the top.

"Oh, I, uh, brought you something."

Amber took the box and slipped the top off, gently. Tyler had made the top into a collar-like contraption for the bear. Amber peered into the box and found a round disk on the bear's lap. She removed it and saw that Tyler had placed a 45 recording of "I Want To Be Where You Are" in with the bear (Julio Iglesias, not Michael Jackson). This melted Amber's heart. From that point on, Kevin, the college guy, was history.

Christmas Day was also the anniversary of Tyler's proposal to Amber. Tyler took a year longer than Amber to graduate from college. After she graduated, Amber got a small apartment, across town from her parents. As a move-in present, she bought herself a tabby cat, Mr. Four Paws.

Tyler would often come home on the weekends and when he did, he spent most of his time at Amber's apartment. Very early in the morning on Christmas day, he tied a diamond ring to Amber's cat and woke her up in the middle of the night. He told her she would have to catch the cat in order to get her ring. Amber jumped up to chase the cat, but catching the cat proved to be no easy feat. Earlier that night she had several drinks and now had the post-drunk woozies. If you're tipsy, you only get drunker after you go to sleep.

Amber's childhood friend, LaShaun, had come over the night before to celebrate Christmas Eve with Amber and Tyler. They had a great time, but Amber still had not developed an alcohol tolerance since her Pink Champale days. LaShaun mixed up several of her special rum and cokes for Amber, leaving her dizzy. LaShaun's bar tending IQ was nil; the drinks were a lot more rum than coke.

After sleeping about a half-hour, Amber had qualified as stoned-cold drunk. She barely managed not to hurt herself as she stumbled after a pissed off and frantic cat in her dark apartment. And anyone who ever owned a cat can imagine how pissed-off a cat, or any other animal, might be if it were being chased around in the middle of the night with miscellaneous shit tied to its collar! The whole thing still made Amber smile as she thought about it. She could remember vividly feeling the pain as she stubbed her toe chasing her cat that night.

To prepare for the move from Austin, Amber and Tyler moved all of their belongings to storage, and they moved into a small, fully furnished studio apartment, also in Lake Hills, just west of Austin. Amber was supposed to stay in the apartment after Tyler left. Tyler was going to move to Iowa, and Amber would follow later. Amber would finish her master's degree faster than they expected; she had gotten a fellowship that would let her quit her job in the mental health center and go to school full time.

When Amber and Tyler were making the plans, they never addressed her idea of pursuing further graduate work. But Amber had made up her mind on her own; it was as if David was giving her new-found strength. The interest that he took in her made her feel more confident and assertive. Up to this point, the men in her life always called the shots. First it was her father. He always laid down the law and that was the way it was. Period. It would have been akin to blasphemy for Amber to disagree. No matter how old she got, Amber's dad had a way of making her feel like she was two-years-old. To some extent, these feelings transferred to Tyler and although Amber recognized this, she sometimes felt it wasn't within her power to do anything her dad or Tyler didn't want her to do.

But David had kind of a rebellious nature and it was rubbing off on Amber. He did whatever the hell he wanted, whenever he wanted and his conscious didn't plague him as Amber's did whenever she disobeyed an authority figure. So Amber decided she would just wait and see. The move was obviously going to happen, but whether it would be a move for both of them was another matter.

During their workouts, Amber found herself beginning to

really confide in David, and he wanted Amber to trust him. She told him about the things going on with her and Tyler. He assured her that if she needed anything, he would be there for her. So after Christmas, Amber didn't wait to discuss things with Tyler, she consulted a lawyer immediately and decided she was going to file for divorce.

It was a much easier decision than she thought it would be, probably because their trip to Louisiana was a disaster. Amber and Tyler had not seen either of their parents since they were married. It wasn't that they didn't want to go home. In fact, Amber was very close to her family, and often tried to visit. Tyler just did not place a particularly high priority on going home to visit. Every time Amber mentioned it, Tyler would find some reason why they could not afford to make they trip. Either he would rationalize about when a better time would be, or he would use any extra money to invest in things that were important to him at the time. The funny thing was Amber could never say no, or she would convince herself she liked whatever new gadget Tyler purchased with their trip money as much as he did.

During their Christmas visit, Amber saw her family and Tyler saw his, mostly separately. Some nights they even slept in different places. Neither one of them mentioned the divorce or their relationship throughout the trip. They attempted to go through the motions of having sex, but it didn't work. Sex had never been great for Amber and now it was worse; all she could see was David and his too sexy physique waiting for her back in

Austin.  He was on her mind more and more.

Amber was shocked when she saw her father.  For the first time in her life, Amber noticed he had aged.  He seemed to have gotten slightly hard of hearing.  When she wanted to take a walk in the mall like they used to, before she left home, he was suddenly out of breath.  This was a big change from the energetic father Amber remembered.  His once smooth skin had wizened and become leathery, and the fire Amber used to imagine she saw dancing his eyes had gone out.  This made Amber worry about him and she vowed that she would never again stay away from home for so long.  Her family needed her, and she needed them.

Just as Amber was shocked to see how her father seemed to have changed since she had married Tyler, her father took one look at her and was not happy with what he saw either.  Later, he told Amber about it.

"Let me see your eyes, sweetie."

He put one of his still strong hands on each shoulder and looked straight into Amber's eyes.  To Amber it felt more like he was looking into the core of her being, into her soul.

"You know," He turned her head side to side as if looking for something.  "A person's eyes can tell you a lot of things, babe.  I can see happiness or sadness. "

"What do you see in mine?"

"I see you been away too long."

Amber knew that meant he didn't like what he saw.  She let the subject drop as her father shifted his gaze to the ground.

"Hmmph!" He shook his head and looked away, letting his arms fall to his sides.

"You know you can always come home, no matter how long you been away." Although he tried to act like he was joking, Amber could hear the sadness in his baritone voice.

Perhaps the incident that put the icing on the cake for Amber was the way Tyler's mom reacted to her. They never exactly got along, but at least they were always civil to each other. Tyler's mom felt her son had gotten the short end of the stick since he reconciled with Amber after their first separation, and she never passed up an opportunity to let Amber know it. Nothing Amber did was right.

Before they went back to Louisiana, Amber got a new haircut, and she liked the way it looked on her and how it made her feel. There was nothing like new shoes or a new haircut to change a person's whole outlook on life. As soon as she saw Tyler's mom, Amber was keenly aware that every inch of her appearance was being assessed, from her head to her toes. Before she had a chance to breathe, Tyler's mom was commenting on her appearance, just as Amber expected she would.

"New hair, huh?" Amber didn't plan on answering; it was an obvious rhetorical question.

"I'm sure it was cute in a magazine, but it doesn't suit you. It makes you look like some dizzy white bitch!"

As she hissed the word 'white' Amber could almost see the fork in her tongue. The words flew out of Tyler's mom's mouth with Tyler looking on and although Amber was quite offended, he didn't say a word.

Amber felt the heat spreading across her face as it became florid with anger. Why did she always have to go there? It was as if she resented Amber for being half a shade lighter than she was. Amber's nostrils flared as she turned on her heels and without saying anything, walked straight out the door and got in her car. At that point, she wished she believed in her grandma's folk tales so she could leave a gris-gris or some other talisman on the mean woman's porch. But she didn't, so she would have to find some other outlet for her anger. Sitting in the car, she could see Tyler peering out the window. He was a coward. Tyler hadn't bothered to stop Amber from leaving. It was the last time Amber set foot in Tyler's parents' home.

# 8

I AM BACK in the familiar place again, standing on the podium. The snake is in front of me and it seems like he is laughing at me. He is talking with no voice and he is saying Marie look into my eyes but I don't want to look and I don't want to be Marie. I just want to be Amber and sleep peacefully for a change. I want to sleep knowing I had good sex and dream good dreams instead.

I look at the snakes eyes anyway; I am powerless in this place because if I weren't I would leave here. I sense with my soul more than I look; my eyes still can't literally see. His eyes are old eyes, knowing eyes, and it is as if I am paper-thin because the snake seems to be looking through me. The drums are still drumming and the people are *still swaying to the music but I am no longer able to make out what they are saying or to see the people individually. I am surrounded but I am the only one there.*

*Inside the snake's eyes I see what I have always seen; I see a big coil stretching through the earth both above it and below it. It is as if the coil is holding the earth on its axis; keeping things in place.*

*The music is rising to a crescendo in the background and I still can't understand the words. I am confused and the snake knows; it is laughing at me. I frown because the snake is talking to me in my father's voice. It is saying that it connects all things and keeps all things in order. I have understood everything up to now but this makes no sense to me. I am feeling suffocated and I look away; sometimes I wish I could stop coming here but I know that I can't.*

*The snake moves toward me and smiles at me some more through those ancient eyes. His tongue flicks out and instead of biting me he kisses me on the lips. I am instantly a new person and I feel released and I can see with my eyes all at once. I look around and I notice that the music has stopped and the people have stopped singing. They are all standing, looking, silent. I feel happy instead of annoyed and confused, but then it is over and everything is gray.*

# 9

BACK IN AUSTIN, Amber was sure of one thing; she didn't want anything from Tyler. He could have everything, except her car. She knew she didn't want money, clothes or even the furniture that they purchased. She had already transferred $5000 from their joint account into a personal account Tyler didn't even know she had. She had learned that lesson well the first time they separated. At that time, she still had this ideal view of marriage, where everything was everything and everyone shared the wealth. So when she left him, after Tyler tried to shoot her, she was caught out there when he closed the bank accounts and left her with no money or credit cards. After she finished crying, all she could do was call home to get money wired to her from her father so she could get a hotel room for the night. Since then, she had always stashed something away for herself just in case.

As she dialed the phone on her first day back from Louisiana, she knew exactly what to expect from Tyler. He was already in his new city, Des Moines. He had already moved on to his new job, so Amber was left by herself in Austin. First, he would be calm, then upset.

"Hey, it's me." She paused. "How's the weather there?"

As expected, Tyler didn't have much to say, but after a few minutes, it was obvious he was not going to be the one to bring up the subject of their relationship.

"Look, I saw a lawyer and filed for divorce." The whole sentence flew out of her mouth in one breath.

"I don't want money or anything, just my car. The money I do want I have already taken." It was said. She waited.

Tyler didn't want to lose face. He answered her, almost too quickly.

"Well, I actually planned to wait until you got here at the end of the semester, you know, after I was settled, and then I was going to ask you for a divorce anyway. It's probably best."
She paused. Amber opened her mouth and closed it again.

"Well, then." And that was it. That was all she could muster.

Amber started to cry as soon as she hung up the phone. She couldn't figure out why; supposedly, this is what she wanted. When she finished crying, she was angry. How dare he think he could let her uproot her life, following him across the country, and then ask her for a divorce! He wanted to wait until he was settled in his new home when it was convenient for him! One more time, he wanted to use her as a support system until he made it through his transition period!

In the middle of Amber's anger, the phone rang. It was Tyler.

"I called the bank, Amber." The anger in his voice seemed to be strangling him. There was no doubt that he was pissed.

"Can you tell me why you took my money?!"

Amber knew it didn't matter that she left him more than half of their cash or that they earned that money together. Tyler just felt everything, including Amber and her money, belonged to him.

Tyler actually told Amber once that the reason he married her was because she was an investment in his future.

"You are going to go places, girl!" At first she thought it was a compliment. "And I am going right along wit' ya!"

Tyler never mentioned love during that conversation. Now Amber could tell he really meant that she was his meal ticket.

Now, listening to him hiss at her through the phone, hearing his rage, she imagined his nostrils flaring and she realized how far he really was from a compliment back then. She was just another milestone, like any other accomplishment. Good education, proper wife, good job, money and not necessarily in that order. He thought he was destined to have it all, and now Amber was screwing up his plan!

Tyler went on an on, until Amber grew tired of listening to his tirade. Amber could hear Tyler's anger and realized that she had the upper hand. Amber didn't bother to hold the phone up to her ear, there was no need to. She knew what the entire phone soliloquy was really about. The last thing she said to him, stopping him in mid sentence was, "Talk to my lawyer."

# 10

NEW YEAR'S EVE. Amber felt she had a lot to celebrate. In prior years, she had stayed home with Tyler instead of going out and celebrating like she wanted. He thought it was not practical to go out on New Year's Eve; that it was too dangerous. But the Tyler era was over. She wanted to party, even if she didn't really feel as if she had anyone to party with.

Amber decided to give Che a call. She always seemed to know what was going on around town. They had worked out their differences before Amber went to Louisiana. This time, Amber decided she would not run from her friendship with Che;

despite Che's misjudgment. They decided to remain friends, despite their differences, with the understanding that Amber had no interest in being involved in any kind of love affair that involved two women.

"Hey, girl. What's up for tonight? You always know where the party is."

"There ain't no major party, " Che said, "But everyone I talked to said they were headed for the club. You know they are having that big New Year deal they have every year. You need to be thinking about having your body there too, you know."

Amber was silent for a minute. It didn't sound like a bad idea at all. But she didn't have a date. Everyone had a date on New Year's Eve. Che seemed to read her mind.

"And you don't need no date, either. Everyone is just coming." Che sucked her teeth. "Tch. Besides, it ain't like you got a man or anything. You threw yours away, girlfriend!"

Now it was Amber's turn to suck her teeth.

"Tchhh," she made sure it was a good, long one.

"You was so busy being a diva, you didn't need him, remember? And you claim you don't do women."

Amber was getting annoyed. Che could be so crass, but at least she got her point across. Before Amber could answer her, there was a knock at her door.

"I gotta go, girl. Lemme call you back."

Amber hung up the phone as she walked toward the door. When she opened it, there was no one there. She looked around, then finally down with her eyes coming to rest on a box wrapped in plain black paper. She grabbed the box, looking around again, without spotting anyone and closed the door.

Amber plopped down on the sofa, which was now free of nacho crumbs, unwrapping the box in the process. "How corny," she said to herself. There was a note in the box with only one letter, a "D", and the time 10 p.m. written on it. Amber smiled to herself as she fingered the note. There was only one "D" and that was David, and he damn sure didn't waste time. Her apartment still smelled like Tyler! The box held a cute little black dress, in the perfect size. The only thing that could have been better was if the dress was one or two sizes too small!

Amber held up the dress and looked at it. It was a great dress, even if she had not purchased it herself. She knew it was similar to something David had seen in an ad and commented on. He seemed to be really into women's fashion and shopping, much to Amber's delight. She was happy, it looked like both of her problems were solved. She had something to wear, and someplace to go. She guessed the time on the note was the time that she was supposed to be where Che said everyone was going - the club. She smiled as she dialed Che's number. Of course she had to rub it in a little! For the first time in a long time, Amber was beginning to feel free.

# 11

AMBER WAS EXCITED as she walked into the club with Che. The place was packed. Like Che said, everyone who was anyone was there. Amber was wearing the surprise black dress. It had only taken her a couple of minutes to get over that she had received the dress as a gift from a married man.

She surveyed her closet and decided the dress was much better than anything else. Besides, it fit perfectly, she looked damn good in it and she knew it!

Amber knew she would be turning heads in her new dress, and it did make her slightly uncomfortable. Although she loved it, Amber was not sure she truly wanted all that extra attention. A part of her felt as if she should be in some type of mourning, but she kept telling herself that marriage was not in the ring that used to be on her finger or on a piece of paper, but in the heart. And it definitely was no longer on her finger; she'd left her wedding band at home. Her heart had already divorced Tyler; there was no reason for her to feel guilty, right?

As Amber and Che approached the club, Amber could not help herself; she looked for David. She couldn't wait to see his face when he saw her in the dress he bought. She imagined his sexy, green eyes caressing her body, from head to her feet, as she knew they would.

Amber and her friends were in the club for almost two hours before she saw David. He was watching her from across the dance floor. When Amber spotted him, he was busy talking to a woman Amber had seen more than once at the gym. David knew that she had filed for divorce, so Amber was expecting him to approach her and ask her to dance. Instead, he just watched her as he usually did. Amber waited, but instead of dancing with her, David danced with someone else.

"Damn!" she thought. "What's his problem?"

As the night wore on, Amber began to feel silly. She must have jumped to conclusions about who sent the dress. Maybe it was just wishful thinking on her part. She just wanted David to be as attracted to her as she was to him. She was disappointed, but she tried to have a good time. At just about midnight, she and Che were standing beside the dance floor and a couple of guys asked them to dance. Amber was pissed off at David, and she really didn't want to dance. Che, on the other hand, was in a good mood for a change.

"Sure!" She chimed her chipper response before Amber had a chance to say no. Amber grabbed Che's arm, stopping her mid-stride as she tried to move to the floor.

"No thanks, we want to finish our drinks first. Maybe later." Amber didn't want to be miserable alone.

Che turned to Amber. "C'mon, live a little. Tcch! He ain't thinkin' 'bout you." Che talked through her teeth. She smiled at the guys who were still standing in front of them. They had their fair share of alcohol and were not about to take no for an answer.

"You feel like ho'in, huh?" She answered Che in the same bitchy tone Che used with her, only with a more hiss. Amber tried to motion the guys away; she really didn't want to dance and their friends were starting to get a little loud as they commented back and forth between themselves.

"Man, they don't want you!" Guy number one didn't seem as drunk as the others.

"Why you say that? Yeah they do. 'Specially that one in the black dress."

"Them girls is too classy for you, man! Leave then alone."

"Naw, man, I'm telling you, they want to dance."

From the corner of her eye, Amber could see another male twosome standing nearby and was thankful they appeared to be listening to her exchange with their troublemaking acquaintances.

One of this other pair turned to Amber.

"Here, honey." He handed her a drink. "You did say wine, right?" He smiled as he handed Che a drink too and turned to their would-be dancer friends.

"Oh, what's up?" You got a problem with my girl?"

Amber and Che both looked surprised but quickly recovered and played along.

"Thanks."

They spoke in unison and sipped their new drinks.

The two troublemaking knuckleheads were drunk, but not that drunk. They were just average Joes. The troublemakers assessed the situation and quickly saw that the new, friendly stranger was a big guy, much bigger than they were.

Amber checked him out, letting her eyes roam over his physique. She could have been saved by worse. He was over six feet two and was very muscular. Not like Tyler, (for some reason Tyler seemed to be Amber's measuring stick), whose barrel chest dominated his body. Everything on this man's body was in perfect proportion. He would never grace the pages of GQ magazine, but he had a distinct handsomeness about him.

Amber noticed he wore a green, silk shirt. He wore it well, too. Some men would think his shirt was feminine. As Che later put it, he oozed. She meant he reeked of sexuality. Some men were just sexy that way, without trying to be. As the two troublemakers backed away, Mr. Friendly moved closer, smiling at Amber.

"You do realize that we have to make this look good, don't you?"

He was close enough to almost breathe his words into Amber's ear, as if he were making love to it.

"Come dance with me."

Amber had forgotten she didn't want to dance. She let herself be led to the dance floor without thinking. For the moment, she put her anger with David at the back of her mind. As they danced, she watched Mr. Friendly, and noticed he was no stranger to the dance floor. He moved very well, especially for a statuesque man. Eventually, the music switched to a slow jam. Amber's first reaction was panic. She usually never danced to slow music. It wasn't appropriate for a married woman to dance to a slow jam with anyone besides her husband.

Before she could protest, Malik pulled Amber into him. Amber noticed his manly, but not overpowering cologne. He smelled good.

"Fuck it, the papers are almost signed anyway." Amber said to herself. She began to relax, letting her body melt into his. She was enjoying herself, and then the music changed tempo again.

"Thanks for the dance." They stopped dancing as soon as the music changed. "By the way, my name is Malik." He turned and walked away, leaving Amber on the dance floor without waiting to find out her name.

Che was still dancing with Malik's friend. By now, they were into each other, openly kissing on the dance floor. Amber watched as Che obviously was doing as much grinding as the guy she was dancing with.

"Damn she's a freak!" she thought. To Amber, the little guy Che' was hugged up to looked like a character straight out of an alien scene on a Saturday morning cartoon. Obviously, Che would kiss anything. Amber was really surprised that Mr. Malik hadn't tried to push up. He'd brought her a drink; they even slow danced. That was definitely a change.

Amber saw Malik at various times throughout the night, but they didn't dance again. Che stayed with her new friend all night, even through the New Year's Eve countdown. Amber knew she couldn't count on riding home with Che. She just hoped her friend had sense enough to use a condom, or at least find out the dude's last name. You can never tell about people, and the man wasn't even as fine as his tall friend, Malik.

When Amber wanted to leave, she realized she hadn't seen David for quite awhile. In fact, she hadn't seen him since she saw him watching her from across the floor, hours ago. They didn't even saw hello. Amber couldn't help but wonder if he had left with that woman she had seen him talking with earlier. She crossed her arms and pouted. Looking around, she didn't see Che at first either. When Amber finally spotted her, she was sitting in a corner with her legs across the lap of her new victim. Che looked like a spider, setting a sweet, sticky trap for her prey. When she got him into her web, she would grab him and pulled him in, instantly killing him in one bite. Poor guy. He looked so happy thinking about the prospect of getting him some for the night that he looked like he might come in his pants right there. Still, Amber didn't quite see why he was attracted to Che, even if he did look like a Muppet show reject. Sure, Che's skin was pretty, but she wasn't exactly what you would call nice looking, and her clothes were tasteless.

Guys were so different, but in a lot of ways, Che was like a guy.

Sometimes, sex alone was enough for her. She had one-night-stands who kept calling her back, even after they found out she was a freak. Sometimes, she called them back. Her explanation for this was even more shocking.

"They come because I got gold in my pussy. I let them stay only if they know how to mine it!"

Amber looked at Che and her unladylike sitting position and frowned.

"Hey, I'm about to turn into a pumpkin. It's time for me to go."

Amber could see the tops of Che's thigh-highs and was sure everyone else could too. If the girl was going to show the world her ass, why couldn't she have worn some decent underwear? Amber wasn't too sure Che even wore panties and didn't want to know. Amber knew what Che's answer would be even before she said it.

"You go ahead, girl. I'll catch up with you later."

"I hope you will," Amber thought. Che didn't know a damn thing about that guy, and she was still going to fuck him!

Amber could see the familiar look in Che's eyes. She was the only Black woman Amber knew who actually picked up men in clubs. Amber never did it. Most of her friends would at least never admit to doing it, even if they had. Che, on the other hand, picked up men in clubs more times than Amber could count, and Amber was sure she had probably picked up women, too. Maybe it was an Austin thing. It just wasn't done that way back in Louisiana.

Amber knew it was Che's choice and Che's life, but she still worried. Her worst nightmare involved Che becoming one of those women on the news, found dead and cut-up in the trunk of an abandoned car or something.

Maybe she watched too much television. Or maybe she was just jealous of Che's uninhibited lifestyle, and afraid of breaking any rules herself.

# 12

AMBER DROVE HOME ALONE. As she did, she was very cautious; New Year's Eve could be a dangerous night. She recalled New Year's Eve back in Louisiana; it was not unusual to hear gunshots fired into the night, sometimes at people.

She lived in an area where the homes were a mixture of apartments, rental homes and one mobile home park. Amber knew when she and Tyler chose the neighborhood that it was not known for its safety, and the walk from the parking lot to her apartment was a long, poorly lit one. She imagined the shadows cast by the trees were people following her, or worse yet, wild animals. There were rumors that there might even still be a mountain lion lurking around. Her thoughts for Che's safety were replaced by thoughts of David. Amber admitted to herself she had hoped he would be attracted to her, too. But it didn't matter that he obviously was not. He had every opportunity to make something happen tonight but hadn't. As a matter of fact, he had ignored her completely. And unlike her friend Che, Amber was not about to make a fool of herself chasing some guy.

Just what was the deal with the hoochie-mama David had spent most of the night talking to? Amber couldn't help feeling a little jealous, but beyond that, she was dying to know who sent her such a great dress! She no longer thought it was David.

When she got into her apartment, Amber began to make herself a cup of tea. She was too keyed up to sleep and the noise outside of her apartment was enough to keep even the soundest sleeper awake. It seemed as if all of the people in her complex were awake. Everyone seemed to be celebrating the new year. Folks didn't seem to have anything to do but stand around the pool in the center of the complex in the middle of the night. Amber noticed as she walked in that several beer bottles were floating in the center of the pool. The water had been turned purple. She later found out one of her neighbors who was upset with the landlord had released an emergency signaling flair into the water, changing its color.

Apparently, he was a pilot and he "borrowed" the emergency flair from work. In his drunken celebration of the new year, he thought that colored water would be amusing. All hell would definitely break loose when the landlord saw that mess! She made a mental note that she would have to move somewhere else where the lighting was at least a little better. Besides, Tyler was the one who chose this cruddy apartment, not her. His cheap ass. Tyler was more concerned with saving a couple of bucks than he was with her safety.

As Amber was waiting for the water for the tea to boil, there was a knock at the door. Glancing at her clock, Amber noticed the time; 2 a.m. "Who the hell could that be?" she wondered. She started toward the door, grabbing the pistol that she kept under her side table. It was a nine-millimeter that Amber knew how to use. Amber started keeping a gun after her relatives convinced her she needed one, being that she insisted on living so far away from home "with that crazy man". They thought it was important that she be able to defend herself the next time Tyler decided to act up. They wanted her to "fight fire with fire"- literally. Amber's uncle purchased the gun for her and even paid for her to go to the shooting range to learn how to use it properly. The gun was his idea of the ultimate birthday gift. He became an advocate of bearing arms since his son, Amber's cousin, John, was shot. Amber was a good shot, and before long, she was comfortable with using the weapon. She knew she would not hesitate to shoot anyone should she feel even the slightest bit frightened.

Once she almost had the opportunity to use it, too. After leaving her aerobics class one day, Amber was walking to her car when a man she didn't recognize approached her.

"Hey, Amber!" he shouted.

Amber hesitated, "I must know him, he knows me." As the stranger got nearer to the car, Amber realized she didn't recognize him, and feeling uncomfortable, she quickly got into her car and drove away.

Afterwards, Amber didn't give the encounter at the gym much thought. Guys were always trying to push up, one way or another. But before long, she noticed she often seemed to see a familiar brown sedan with California plates in several places around town. Wherever she was, the brown car seemed to be too. At first she thought it was a coincidence or that she was imagining it. Then she began to get uneasy.

Around this same time, the town of Killeen, which was not too far from Austin, had experienced a string of murders. Several young women had been found dead, either in their apartments or cut up and stuffed into the trunks of their cars. The police speculated that all of the murders were related; they said it was a strong possibility they were committed by someone who the victims knew. As a result, residents in the area were on pins and needles. Everyone was being extra cautious, including Amber. That's when she started to carry the gun in her glove compartment. A lawyer friend advised her to go ahead and carry the gun but without the ammunition clip in it. If the police stopped her, she was to say she was on her way home from the range. As long as the clip wasn't in the gun, she should be okay.

The local serial killer's fifth victim had just been found and again Amber was on her way home from the gym. As she was getting in her car, with her door still open, Amber looked up. To her surprise, the same weird guy who she had spotted before was walking toward her, calling her name.

"Hey Amb—", he shouted.

Amber flipped her glove compartment open and loaded the magazine into it in virtually one move.

"What the fuck do you want!" She was too angry to think. She pointed the gun right at the guy's crotch.

"Back the fuck UP!" she yelled. He was too surprised to do anything but put his hands in the air and stop dead in his tracks. Amber was sitting, and he was standing. Even if she were not such a great shot, he would surely suffer forever if she pulled the trigger.

Amber got in her car, slammed the door, and sped away. She was angry, and as she drove away, she noticed the stranger had gotten into the same brown sedan that she had noticed following her before. He was pulling out of the parking lot, too. She knew, without a doubt, had that guy taken one more step in her direction, she would have fired the gun. Amber drove all the way to the nearest police station, keeping one eye on the dusty brown car in her rear-view mirror. When she arrived, the car didn't follow her into the precinct parking lot. Instead, it drove right by. Amber was fine until the desk cop spoke.

"Can I help you Miss?" At that point, she lost all of her composure and started to sob uncontrollably. When she finally calmed down enough to relate the incident to the police, minus the part about the gun, the police officer was of little help.

"Well, Miss, there's not much we can do. He didn't threaten you with bodily harm, did he?"

Amber was shocked and angry. Since Texas didn't have an anti-stalking law, the police told her there was nothing that they could do. The stranger hadn't threatened her or tried to hurt her. She got the impression the whole thing somehow amused the police. It was as if the police felt she was "just another hysterical woman". Since that incident, Amber kept her gun loaded and in easy reach whenever she was inside her apartment. It made her feel not so alone knowing she could possibly defend herself if necessary.

As she turned to respond to the early morning knock on her door, she instinctively picked up the gun. Without moving toward the door, Amber called out, "Who is it?"

"It's me, Amber. Are you going to let me in or what?" Amber put her gun down. It was David! Damn! What was he doing at her place at this time of night? She couldn't help it. She was excited. Amber made a mental note to keep her cool as she opened her door.

"Hey, David. What are you doing here?"

"Well," he said, "I was thinking about you and decided to drop by."

"What a line! If you were thinking about me why didn't you act like it at the club? Come on in. I'm having some tea, would you like some?" Amber stepped away from the door so David could come in.

"No, I just want to talk," he answered. Amber's excitement grew as he crossed his legs on her couch.

"I'm having problems with my wife, and I needed someone to talk to. I guessed that you might understand since you are going through similar problems yourself."

David was too smooth for words, and it was working on Amber. Their conversation wandered to things other than David's relationship with his wife. They talked about Amber and Tyler, with David swearing that if he had been in Tyler's shoes, he definitely would have done things differently. Amber was charmed and thrilled; she was now sure that David was interested in her too.

They talked until dawn.

"Well, what do you plan to do for the rest of your winter break, Amber?"

"I have until January 15. I'm going to hang around and sort out my life."

So much had happened in the past two weeks, Amber felt the need to take some time to herself to get back in shape for the upcoming semester; it would be her last one. She had quit her regular job at the mental health center and got a job as a teaching assistant at the psychology department at the school. Amber was also looking forward to hearing from the graduate schools she applied to. She knew for sure she still wanted to get that Ph.D. in industrial Psychology.

"I can understand the need for a break, Amber. Do you ski?"

"I sure do. I learned how to ski in high school, on my senior trip. I love it!"

Amber was one of those people who had never been a beginner on the ski slopes. She tried it on a dare on her senior trip and loved it although none of her friends skied. They accused her of "trying to be white" because she actually took up the dare and had the nerve to admit she liked it. Her father told her she was crazy for trying.

"Black folks don't have no business sliding on ice," he used to say. Amber dismissed his comments as being old fashioned, but she went skiing only once or twice after he made them. It was easier not to go than to hear people rant and rave.

Tyler thought skiing was dangerous and refused to try, so Amber stopped skiing. If he were hurt while skiing, he might be grounded from flying. He didn't want to take the chance. Although he felt this way, Amber noticed that he watched the ski competitions religiously. Tyler admitted that it looked like fun, but he just refused to try it. He took all sorts of precautions not to lose his pilot's license, and often gave up new experiences or fun in the process. After his car accident, he lost his pilot's license anyway but still hadn't skied.

David put his hand on Amber's knee, sensing that Amber's

mind was somewhere else.

" I know a great little ski resort and lodge run by the Mescalero Apache Indians in Northern New Mexico. We could get away, Amber.  It would be easier for both of us to sort things out that way."

Amber was surprised by the invitation.  She hadn't expected it, but David was so convincing. And tempting.

"What about your wife?" Amber couldn't help asking.   How would he pull this off?  He would obviously have to lie, but what lie could he tell that would allow him to be able to get away for a week with another woman?  There was no way in hell Amber could have pulled something like this off with Tyler.  She just wasn't that good a liar.

"You let me worry about that.  Can you be ready to go on Monday?"

It was not within Amber's powers to turn him down.  She didn't care what happened; she was going to do what she wanted for a change.  She was going skiing!  Amber and David agreed he would be back at her place at 8 a.m.  She would be packed and ready to go, no questions asked.

Amber walked David to the door.  They kissed; it happened so naturally, just like it was something that occurred every day. Neither one of them paused like people do on TV, waiting for the good-bye kiss to come; they didn't have to wonder who would start first.  David took his index finger and gently lifted Amber's face toward his own, pulling her toward him in the process.  His mouth was as sensual as the rest of his body. Amber felt as if his lips were caressing hers. She closed her eyes as she let his softly probing tongue part her lips, not even realizing that she was holding her breath. It was as if the kiss echoed; it took Amber a minute to realize it was over. The kiss made Amber dizzy; that was a first.

Amber was intoxicated by the whole thing; it was not lost on David; he was charming and he knew it.

"By the way, I'm glad the dress fit. It looked great on you." David turned and walked away. Amber just smiled. She was in la-la land and knew it was best not to answer. She wouldn't be able to gather any words together that would make sense.

# 13

THE SNAKE IS *staring at me again. His kiss did not hurt, but now my eyes are working and I can see. I know that the music has stopped and the people are staring, but I can't see them like I want to. I almost liked it better when I was seeing with my mind. It was somehow safer.*

*Now I am beginning to see other things inside the snake's eyes. I see myself caught in a storm, severe, like a Texas storm. In fact, a tornado has just passed and it is in front of me. The snake is again speaking inside my mind in my Daddy's voice, "Soon come," he is saying. I don't know what he thinks is coming. Inside the snake's eyes, I see myself look behind me and I see another tornado. I want to run. I am running and looking for shelter. I wonder where my daddy is? I am* running and looking for him because I know he can save me from the tornado. "Soon come, " The snake says again, but this time in my Nana's voice. Well, I don't plan to be here when it does. Anybody who has ever watched a horror movie knows that black folks don't stick around for danger. But that doesn't explain why they always are killed first. This is funny to me and I laugh as I continue to look for shelter. Then I run more because I know that there is a third storm behind the two that I have already seen.

I see my family standing together. I think they are my family because I see my daddy, my mother, Nana, and my Daddy's daddy. That part is kinda funny to me too because I have never even really met my Daddy's daddy, just seen his picture. These other people must be related too. This is a logic problem, like on the GRE. I laugh to myself as I think about the logic problem and watch them all smile at me with their arms outstretched, beckoning me to them. Everything is calm where they are. But what fun is that? I am not ready to go there and I am debating what to do while I am thinking about the two tornadoes waiting for me. They wait while I debate and then they begin to fade away.

# 14

AMBER CALLED CHE. She had barely slept a wink thinking about her trip with David. She was excited but she was not sure she had made the right decision. What would people say? Everyone knew she was still married, and people knew David was married too. The more she thought about it, the more she was sure she didn't really give a damn what people thought. She had been doing what she was supposed to do for 26 years now. It was time for a change. Che picked up the phone on the fourth ring.

"Hey girl, guess what? I'm going skiing." Amber relayed the whole story to Che. She knew Che would support her decision to be daring. Che was the traditional rebel; she would understand.

Che listened to all of Amber's story with mixed feelings.

"I'm not sure that this is such a good idea," said Che.

'Excuse me?"

"You don't really know a whole lot about this guy, Amber. I mean, he could be a weirdo or something."

Amber was confused and livid. Any other time, Che would be the one who reminded her how much she avoided taking risks.

"You're letting your life pass you by," she would say. "You never know unless you try." Now here she was, telling Amber to be more careful!

"You're just jealous!" Amber yelled into the phone. "For a change, I'm the one having fun, and you can't take it. This isn't the first time you have been jealous of me either! I'll talk to you when I get back! "

Actually, Amber was right. Che was jealous. Everything always seemed to go right for Amber. First, she had one Prince Charming who she threw away. Then, she gets another one. It was too much like a fairy tale, and Che couldn't take it. She wanted her own fairy tale for a change. Everyone liked Amber. She was pretty and smart. It was just too much. Now she had a guy who wanted to take her away for a fabulous weekend. Why was it that Amber got all the good ones?

"It's your life, girlie." Whatever Amber wanted to do was fine with her.

"Why did I bother to tell you this anyway?" Amber was

disgusted. She didn't wait for Che to say anything else. She slammed the phone down and began to look for her suitcase.

# 15

AS SHE SAT ON THE PLANE next to David, she kept pinching herself. Things just seemed to be happening so quickly. David had shown up at her place bright and early, just like they had planned. They were flying to El Paso and then driving to the ski resort. David explained to her that they would be flying in a private plane owned by a friend of his. They had to fly into El Paso because it was the site of the nearest airfield where they were authorized to land. "Talk about living a fairy tale!" Amber thought to herself. "This is just like something that would happen in the movies." She just hoped it wouldn't turn out to be a horror movie. She had to keep pinching herself; after Che's reaction, she hadn't told anyone where she was going!

One thing Amber knew for sure was David was full of surprises. Some of the stories he used to share with her about his life were definitely remarkable, but this one took the cake. It was obviously true because here she was, sitting in the smallest plane she had ever been in, flying to someplace she had never heard of. From the sound of the name of the hotel, she was definitely in for an interesting and romantic weekend.

According to David, his parents were very wealthy and eccentric. Once, he claimed they took him and his sister out of school for two years, so the family could sail around the world together. He was eight at the time. Supposedly, the trip was cut short because the family's yacht got too close to the Liberian shoreline. At the time, Liberia was going through some sort of civil uprising. As a result, the boat was taken. The family, David included, were "detained". They were rescued by some guy dressed as a missionary, after David's father contracted malaria. They were then sent to England where they stayed for four months while David's father recovered.

When David first told her this story, Amber was really skeptical, thinking he had a very overactive imagination. Besides, he didn't seem worldly enough to her to have been to all the places he claimed. She knew a roughneck when she saw one, and David was definitely the real thing. Unrefined, so to speak. Now Amber wasn't so sure what to believe. He claimed to have a friend with a plane and here they were! Maybe the other stories were true, too.

Amber and David arrived at the Inn of the Mountain Gods very late at night. The drive from the airfield had taken them almost 3 hours because of icy roads. Even at night, the place was very beautiful. Amber felt as if it were just what she needed to take her mind off things.

Amber was nervous and David must have sensed it; he ordered wine from room service as soon as they checked in. At this point, Amber was starting to have renewed doubts about taking this trip. She was remembering the serial killer back in Austin and began feeling silly for having disappeared without telling anyone where she was headed. What if something happened to them or if David turned out to be a nut? No one would even know where to begin looking for her.

Eventually, the wine they were drinking began to take effect. Amber had come a long way from her Pink Champale days, but it still didn't take much to make her tipsy. Soon, she was more comfortable and sitting close to David didn't make her as nervous as he did a few minutes before.

"So, do you like the place?" David asked. "I found it a long time ago. I've lived in Texas a long time, you know." Amber smiled, but before she could answer, David moved closer and kissed her. First on her lips, then moved slowly down her neck. Normally, Amber would have resisted such a bold move, but the wine gave her an excuse to be just a little more daring. Instead of protesting, she responded more passionately than she ever thought she could. "What the hell! No one can see, and besides, he is paying for the weekend," she thought to herself.

Amber let David go where he wanted. Before long, they were making love. For the first time, Amber enjoyed herself. David seemed to know exactly where to touch and what to do. All of Amber's experience had been with Tyler, and he was never concerned about her pleasure. When she was with Tyler, Amber just wanted the whole thing to be over. Tyler had always seemed to be more concerned with getting his own rocks off that Amber felt forgotten about.

With David, it was different. Almost like they literally fit together perfectly. With anyone else, she might have been embarrassed at some of the things David attempted to do to her, but instead she enjoyed every move that was made. It was definitely an education for Amber. She had only read about some of the things they did that night, or at least only heard about them from Che. They didn't get to ski much that weekend. Most of the time, they just stayed in the room.

# 16

THE WEEKEND IN PARADISE ended quickly. When she returned home, the first thing she did was to go see Che. She knew she had to talk to someone to help sort certain things out. She was pretty much over her guilt; she had to be or she would go crazy. Tyler just didn't matter anymore, but she had to hear someone else agree with her. David made her feel better about herself in one weekend than Tyler had in 10 years.

Che was frantic when she saw Amber driving up to her apartment. She met her at the door.

"Girl, where have you been? You left without telling anyone where you were going!" Amber smirked at her friend. She knew

Che wanted the scoop on what happened between her and David.

"You were so busy being nasty to me on the phone, I didn't have a chance to tell you about any of the details," she answered. Amber knew Che was jealous, and she was dying for a chance to rub it in.

"I know you gave up the panties, but never mind that, you need to check yourself. Tyler's back in town, and he was asking where you were. I thought you said it was over between you two?"

Che explained that while Amber was enjoying her blissful weekend with Prince Charming, Tyler returned to Austin looking for Amber. When he didn't find her at home or at any of her other usual spots, he had asked everyone he could find where Amber went. Apparently, Che mentioned to him "accidentally-on-purpose" that she heard Amber went somewhere on vacation with another man! For Che, it was actually more on purpose than anything else. She was glad Tyler was back. Amber needed some rain on her parade. Maybe he and Amber would get back together and Amber would be her normal self again. At least Che would know what to expect from Amber then.

On one hand, Amber was surprised to hear Tyler even gave a damn about where she was, but she should have guessed he would try and have the last word on things.

"How much has he found out?" she wondered. With his temper, he was so unpredictable. There was no telling what he would do.

Amber thought about Che's news; she didn't really have time

to be pissed off at Che for spilling the beans. If Tyler was still in town, she needed to know where he was. David should know that he might be a problem. But Amber still couldn't risk calling David at home. She didn't have his phone number anyway. Amber couldn't believe that one fantastic weekend led to so much drama, but she wasn't about to let Che see her worry. She would have to deal with this stuff later.

" I have no idea why he was here, Che, and I am not about to sweat it." Amber tried to make herself sound as convincing as possible, but Che didn't buy it. She wanted to make sure she rubbed in every bit of information she had discovered. While Amber and David were away, she had uncovered more dirt than Amber realized.

"Guess who I ran into while I was getting my nails done?" Che asked with a sneer on her face. At this point, Amber didn't really care. She needed to leave and figure out what she was going to do, but Che was not about to let her off easy.

"David's wife was getting her nails done the same time I was. And guess what?" Now Amber was curious, and Che knew it. She wanted to play with Amber a little more. She had a long vindictive streak that would not let her resist the opportunity. Amber was the one in trouble for a change.

"Not that I was listening, but I heard her tell her nail tech she wanted to do her nails differently. She asked her for fiberglass with a French manicure." Amber looked at Che.

"So what? What's the big deal with that? Lots of people

wear their nails that way!" Amber was getting annoyed. Che was obviously holding back information, but she didn't want to appear too eager.

"I heard her tell the tech that she wanted them that way because her husband liked them that way. Don't you wear yours like that?" Amber caught her breath. Che was trying to make something out of nothing.

"You know what else? "

Che was not done. Now she was about to rub salt into the wound.

"She said her husband was out of town for business, but they had a special night out planned as soon as he got back. I thought you said he told you they were breaking up, and she was supposed to be going back to Florida?"

Amber couldn't believe it. David lied to her. She had trusted him, and he had lied. She should have known better. He also told her he and his wife hadn't slept together in over a month. That was probably a lie too!

Che watched as waves of emotion flooded Amber's face. She wasn't finished. Che was saving the creme-de-la-creme for last.

"Oh yeah, did you know she is three weeks pregnant?"

Amber felt as if someone had punched her in the stomach.

"Yeah, I knew that."

She was not about to let Che see how hurt and disappointed she was.

"I gotta go, I'll have to catch you later."

Amber grabbed her bag and headed for the door, trying not to look unhappy. Che, on the other hand, was feeling very chipper. She knew she had thrown a wrench in the works; Amber's Prince Charming had begun to look more and more like a toad, and she loved it. Maybe now she wouldn't be so self righteous and judgmental toward her.

"Okay," she said with smile on her face. "Maybe we can get together and do the girl's night out thing this week!"

Amber smiled weakly. "Sure, Whatever. I'll call you." She backed out of the door like Che would stab her in the back, turned and headed for her car.

In her car, Amber choked back tears. She hadn't asked him to leave his wife or anything, and he damn sure didn't mention anything about a baby. Why would David have his wife get her nails done like hers? She guessed that she should be flattered about this part, but why the lies? What else was a lie? And this thing with Tyler being in town, looking for her like a crazy man, what was with that?

"Damn, I cheated on my husband. It's all David's fault," she thought. "What now?' Adultery was a sin in every religion she could think of. If she were still Catholic, she would already be in the confessional booth. One good thing about Catholicism, it let you repent immediately for your sins. She was definitely doomed to fire and brimstones now!

Amber kept thinking about David. He obviously didn't care about her. She was going to give him a piece of her mind. As a matter of fact, she was going to fuck him over, before he fucked her again. Instead of heading for her apartment, Amber turned her car in the direction of the neighborhood she and Tyler used to live in. She was going to drop in on Mr. David and his happy family. She was going to check out the situation for herself.

Amber pulled over at the next gas station she saw and headed for the pay phone, immediately dialing information. It would be easy to get David's number, as long as it was listed. His last name was Koppler; how many David Kopplers could there be in Austin? If she called and his wife answered, she would know David had lied to her.

"Hello?" There was no mistaking a woman's voice was answering the phone. Amber was caught off guard. She could hear laughter in the background.

"Hello? Who is it?" The woman sounded annoyed. Amber opened her mouth to speak and nothing came out. She hung up the phone.

"Damn!" She said out loud. What was she going to do now? If she called the right number, David obviously had lied.

Amber got back into a car and once again headed to David's house. She was less than five miles away. She had no idea what she would do once she arrived; she was too angry to think rationally.

While they were in college, LaShaun told her that if you really wanted to get to a man, mess up his car. At the time, it was the most ridiculous thing Amber ever heard, but now it sounded real good. Back then, LaShaun was angry with some guy she was dating because he told everyone about the present she gave him for his birthday. Amber was never quite able to figure out what that present was. At the time, she possessed a limited sexual imagination and could not, for the life of her, figure out what to do with cotton candy and whipped cream. The poor guy had his car painted recently and it was his pride and joy. Amber actually accompanied LaShaun to where the guy's car was parked, without knowing what she had planned to do. She watched, astonished, as LaShaun poured syrup and whipped cream all over the car, and then stuck the cotton candy to the mess she had created. LaShaun topped off her strange car sundae by keying the guy's car, first up one side and then down the other. Amber was shocked. She knew people who had gotten killed for less.

As she approached David's house, she realized the car thing probably wasn't a good idea in this case. David's car was a piece of shit. It seemed to be the only thing he didn't care about. He would probably thank her for helping her get money from his insurance company. Instead, Amber just sat outside of David's house and waited. She watched to see if she could spot movement in the house, or if someone would come outside.

After about 10 minutes, Amber left her car and walked up to the door. She was so angry; she didn't bother with the doorbell. She kicked the door so hard she heard it splinter. Nothing. She kicked it again and could hear a dog yapping on the other side.

"Maybe I called the wrong number," She thought. She was

suddenly aware of the possibility of her former neighbors seeing her outside David's door, acting like an idiot. She turned and started toward her car, glancing over her shoulder more than once to make sure no one came to the door. Maybe they thought she was selling something.

"I must have called the wrong number."

Amber didn't start her car immediately; she waited, silent, noticing the gray, January sky. A car passed too quickly as Amber flicked her now tired eyes to her dashboard clock. She realized she had left Che's house over an hour ago and was no longer mad. She would deal with Miss Che and Mr. David later.

# 17

ONE WEEK AND TWO HOURS.  Amber could not believe it had been that long since she had heard from David.  He wasn't even in the gym at their normal hour.  Che kept asking her what was going on, but Amber found she was no longer in the information-sharing mood.  She didn't feel much like being open with anyone, least of all with Che.  Che seemed to get too much pleasure from other people's pain, and Amber was slowly figuring out there were some things that still couldn't be shared, especially with another woman, and definitely not with Che.  Che made things more complicated too; she sometimes acted as if she were jealous of Amber or David or both, depending on how you looked at the situation. Although they had their little talk about Che's bisexuality, Amber still felt as if Che had not totally given up on the idea of them being together.

Amber was in a nasty mood, she was alternating between feeling used by both David and Che. "What's going on with me?" she wondered. Things were way out of control. It was Thursday, and she had heard neither hide nor hair of Tyler's whereabouts either. Her sixth sense told her he probably just went back to work. Besides, he could not possible have too much time off from his new job.

Although she didn't really feel like it, Amber felt obligated to go to the club. If nothing else, going might help to release some tension. Secretly, she hoped David would be there. She knew many people would be returning to school, so she was expecting to see lots of college students.

Amber drove to the club, picking up Che on the way. She preferred to be the driver, especially since there was no telling how Che would act when they were there. If she drove, she knew she would never have to depend on anyone to get home. In Louisiana, her father used to tell her to always be sure she had car fare home, and to this day, she always did, one way or another.

As they walked into the club, Amber recognized a few people she knew. She and Che also recognized the presence of the usual "mud-sharks", as they called them. Usually on R&B night, most of the white people stayed away, but there were always the few who just seemed to be "out to catch", and tonight was no exception. Folks would joke and say that these few white people wanted them "some dark meat". Everyone knew where to find it, especially on Thursday nights. Che had an on-going joke about Blacks who socialized with the whites at the club. The "mud-sharks" were usually white women, hanging around Black men or so it seemed.

"Girl, those folks be sticking they spoons in the milky cereal!" Che had stole that from the lyrics of some rap artist to alert Amber when an interracial "incident" was happening, and it soon became one of their favorite lines. It didn't matter if anyone else heard her, usually, they would have no clue what she was talking about. It was their own secret code. Tonight, Amber and Che were both kinda mellow, sitting and watching the other club-goers as they sipped their drinks.

"Oop, brother alert! Check it out! Check it out!" Amber looked up, and recognizing the guy as a student from campus.

"Ope, but he is dippin' girl. Too bad!" He was an undergraduate; Amber had seen him around. There were so few Blacks on campus, both undergraduate and graduate, that everyone knew each other. This guy was a football player, and Amber didn't remember being too impressed by him. When she first started school, he didn't know Amber was married and had asked her out. "What a dumb jock!', she'd thought. Even though she turned him down, he followed her around the Student Union for weeks, like a puppy.

Amber looked at him dancing with his white girl, she noticed her dirty-blond hair appeared to be very stringy and unkempt. Amber often ignored Che's jokes, but for some reason the sight of this young brother, with drink in hand, dancing with Miss-Stringy-Hair made her angry. He would be all over that girl tonight in the club, but tomorrow they would act like they didn't know each other. Just like David had obviously done to her! "Some nerve!" she thought.

Amber stood up.

"You know what? I suddenly feel like dancing."

She grabbed her skirt between her thumb and forefinger on each side, doing a slight shimmy as she pulled it back into place, just above her thigh-high multicolored boots. "Watch this!" she said, almost to herself.

Without so much as two seconds thought, Amber approached the Jock and Miss-Stringy-Hair. They were barely dancing, really just swaying in front of each other. Amber looked on, trying to figure out which of the two had less rhythm. A few seconds before, she saw him kissing the girl on her neck. Amber approached the couple so the girl had her back to Amber.

The Jock looked surprised as he watched Amber approach. His surprise softened into a smile as he saw Amber come straight at him. "What are you doing with THAT?" she mouthed, indicating the girl he was dancing with. The music was too loud to communicate any other way. The Jock continued to look at Amber, dumbfounded. "Get rid of her, I want to dance!"

Amber crossed her arms and waited. Amber's friends looked on, surprised. Usually, Amber was so polite and proper, now here she was, causing a scandal.

"What is she doing?!"

"I don't know, girl."

"She oughta just leave 'em alone. He ain't thinking about her.

They all watched, surprised, as the Jock whispered into his partner's ear. She turned around, looked Amber up and down, frowning. As she did, she attempted the annoyed-sister-neck-roll. Amber stood her ground, with her hand on her hip as the girl turned and walked away, passing her as she left the dance floor. She came two fractions of an inch short of bumping Amber as she left.

Amber smiled and stepped up to take Miss Stringy Hair's spot, in front of her new dancing partner. Her friends looked on with amazement. After about two minutes of dancing, the Jock tried to talk to Amber.

"What happened to Vanilla Ice, your library friend?" Confused, Amber continued dancing. Did he mean David? She wasn't aware anyone noticed her with David on campus. They had only met in the library, in Amber's research room.

Suddenly, her game was no longer fun. She was bored anyway, and turned and walked back to her table, leaving her partner standing on the dance floor, looking dazed. He threw his hands up in the air as if to say, "What the-!" while Amber left him standing there with a dumb look on his face, with everyone looking on.

"Why did you do that?" Che asked, astonished.

"I just felt like being a bitch! And you know what, it felt good!"

Amber was tired of being taken advantage of. Her father used to tell her that shit rolled down hill. She wasn't about to be the one at the bottom. She was tired of being nice and smiling all the time. She noted that although she knew she should feel guilty, she felt like someone lifted a load off of her shoulders.

"Besides he didn't have no business with Miss Stringy Hair anyway."

Amber dropped Che off on her way home. For once, she didn't pick anyone up. Che was going home to actually sleep in her own bed for a change.

"What happened to Ms. Goody Goody?" Che's face was smug. She felt like picking at Amber.

"Mind your business, just having a little fun, that's all!"

Che was really surprised at her friend, but she didn't push further. It was about time she stopped putting up a big front anyway. She tried to act as if nothing ever fazed her.

Unlike Amber, Che had seen David in the past week. She could tell Amber felt David used her; if she were in Amber's shoes she would feel used. It was obvious she was taking it out on the folks around her, she didn't need a psychology degree to be able to tell that much.

Amber was changing since her split with Tyler. Although she

told Che on more than one occasion that her split was just a minor change in her life and didn't matter, Che guessed the icing on the cake was David's mysterious disappearance.

Without Amber's knowledge, Che had visited David at his job. Two days after he and Amber returned from their weekend getaway, Che decided to go and check out Amber's "Mr. Wonderful" for herself. Before David, Amber and Che seemed to spend more time together. Since the two of them started hanging out, Amber seemed to have less time for Che, and she was more secretive than ever.

David worked for a small brokerage firm in downtown Austin. While they were getting their nails done, his wife had blabbed about his supposed big sales and commissions. Che didn't mention that part to Amber. She listened, filing the information away for later use. Later came sooner than she expected. Che called David's office, asking for an appointment. She was a really good actress and the secretary didn't ask any questions, just putting Che on David's calendar without hesitation.

"He's too good to be true, " Che thought to herself as she got ready for her appointment. She planned to find out just how much of a dog Mr. David really was. She wanted to be able to show Amber first hand what David was really made of. David met Che in the waiting room.

"I'm sorry, you're Che, right? Amber's friend? What can I do for you?"

Che smiled at David as she followed him into his office. He

was trying to play the role, like he really didn't know who she was. He knew damn well she hadn't come for investment advice. As they walked through the door, Che boldly closed it behind her. Instead of taking the seat he offered her, Che stood up. She remembered the stuff Amber had told her about the psychology of position. She remembered that the desk would act like a barrier between them. She wanted to be in control so she wanted her head to be taller than his. She wasn't sure she believed all of the things Amber had told her, but standing up sure made her feel like she had in control, so it couldn't hurt.

"So, I hear you're seeing my friend, Amber."

David looked uncomfortable, and Che loved it. She could tell t by standing up she had thrown him off guard, and she had every intention of keeping the upper hand in the conversation.

"Excuse me," he said. "I don't know what you are talking about. Amber and I used to be neighbors."

Che couldn't believe it. David was standing in her face telling her a boldfaced lie! He was taking up her time with Amber and lying about it. Che slowly walked toward David, stepping onto his side of the desk. It had made him even more uncomfortable. As she had moved closer, invading his "intimacy zone", as Amber called it, David stepped back. There was nowhere for him to go.

"I'm not here to talk about her anyway."

Che was wearing a tan London Fog trench coat. As she moved closer to David, she had untied the sash and let the coat fall open. David saw she didn't have much on underneath. He had sat in his chair and Che stepped in front of him.

"Amber and I are really good friends, and we like to share."

Che loved to see men squirm, it turned her on. Her black teddy with thigh-high stockings was in full view. David had been motionless; he had leaned back in his chair, taking all of Che into view. Che took his arm and placed it around her waist, forcing David's face close to her abdomen. He had smiled as he began to reach for Che.

"I see," he had said, obviously at loss for words. Che had sat back on his desk as David began kissing her stomach, timidly at first, then with more conviction. She had smiled as he began to move downward, and as he did, Che had leaned further back and opened her legs, gently guiding his head in the direction she wanted.

Suddenly, David had stopped and rolled his chair backwards, moving away from Che.

"You slut!" David's voice was full of contempt. "How dare you come in here like this, thinking I would want you or fall for your bullshit!" Che had opened her mouth to speak, but David wasn't finished.

"Some friend you are! Sure, Amber and I are friends. But even if we weren't, I wouldn't get with you if someone paid me to!" His words hit home, Che felt as if she had been slapped in the face. She had stood up, tying her belt as she headed for the door.

"Fuck you. I've heard about you, and I know you are a piece

of shit, even if Amber doesn't." She had jerked the door open and stepped into the hallway.

"I'm sorry I couldn't be of more help, Miss Johnson." David lowered his voice and smirked as he watched Che storm away.

Now on the way home from the club with Amber, Che remembered her encounter with David. He was obviously no good, but she was still jealous. Hopefully he would go away soon, and she and Amber could go back to the way their friendship was pre-David.

As Amber dropped her off, Che couldn't help but imagine what it would have been like if things continued the way they had been going that day in David's office. She knew he really wasn't the gentleman he professed to be, and she could appreciate getting down and dirty in any setting. Maybe she would find out eventually. Che knew a dog when she saw one.

After dropping Che at her door, Amber continued on home. She was really surprised at Che's apparent good attitude for a change. Usually, if she had fun, Che didn't. It was as if she couldn't stand to see Amber have a good time. She noticed that tonight Che seemed to be in an usually good mood and smiled more than usual. It was as if she had her own private secret. Che even laughed with her when she left that dufus alone on the dance floor.

As Amber unlocked her apartment door, she continued to contemplate the night's events, including David's apparent absence at the club. Not only did he ignore her completely for a week, he also seemed to be avoiding her.

"That's okay," she told herself. "He wasn't even that good!" But she knew she was lying. She thought about David day and night, often reliving their first night together in full detail and color. She was still thinking about him as she opened her door, so much so, in fact, that it took several minutes for the scene that confronted her to register.

Amber looked around. Her apartment was a shambles! Her dresser drawers had been emptied onto the floor, and things were strewn everywhere. It didn't seem as if anything was missing, but the mirror in the bedroom was cracked and someone had written the word "Bitch" across it in lipstick. Even her jewelry was dumped onto the floor. Amber surveyed the damage.

"When it rains, it pours". She bent down to pick up the remains of a necklace her father gave her for Christmas. It was a beaded necklace with a gold ankh on the end; the Egyptian symbol of life. It wasn't very expensive, in fact it was tacky everywhere else but back home, but it was her absolute favorite piece of jewelry. Whoever ransacked her apartment sure knew how to hit a person where it hurt. Sitting on the floor, Amber held the ankh, and looked at the remaining beads strewn around her, scattered across the floor. She felt as if her life had slowly began to unravel, in the same manner in which the beads had come off their string. Slowly, she began to gather the beads together, and as she did, she started to cry.

# 18

THE SNAKE IS *staring at me again. His kiss did not hurt, but now my eyes are working and I can see. I know that the music has stopped and the people are staring, but I can't see them like I want to. I almost liked it better when I was seeing with my mind. It was somehow safer.*

*Now I am beginning to see other things inside the snake's eyes. I see myself caught in a storm, severe, like a Texas storm. In fact, a tornado has just passed and it is in front of me. The snake is again speaking inside my mind in my Daddy's voice, "Soon come," he is saying. I don't know what he thinks is coming. Inside the snake's eyes, I see myself look behind me and I see another tornado. I want to run. I am running and looking for shelter. I wonder where my daddy is? I* am running and looking for him because I know he can save me from the tornado. "Soon come" the snake says again, but this time in my Nana's voice. Well, I don't plan to be here when it does. Anybody who has ever watched a horror movie knows that black folks don't stick around for danger. But that doesn't explain why they always are killed first. I am still looking for shelter. Then I run more because I know that there is a third storm behind the two that I have already seen.

I see my family standing together. I think they are my family because I see my daddy, my mother, Nana, and my Daddy's daddy. That part is kinda funny to me because I have never even really met my Daddy's daddy, just seen his picture. These other people must be related too. This is a logic problem, like on the GRE. I laugh to myself as I think about the logic problem and watch them all smile at me with their arms outstretched, beckoning me to them. Everything is calm where they are. But what fun is that? I am not ready to go there and I am debating what to do while I am thinking about the two tornadoes waiting for me. They wait while I debate with myself. I wonder why I am having the same dream as before and they begin to fade away.

# 19

AMBER WAITED until morning to clean up the mess in her apartment. As she picked up the pieces, she thought about the things the policeman told her last night. She was sure Tyler was the culprit. There was no sign of forced entry, so who else could it be? And with his temper, there was no telling what he might do. The police had been very condescending; Amber was surprised they even answered the call so quickly. But Austin was different than Baton Rouge. They had no idea she was Black. She could tell by the surprise on the officer's face when she opened the door. "What's the matter, am I on the wrong side of I-35?" she thought.

Back home, if a burglary call came into 911 from a Black neighborhood, the police would take their own sweet time answering it. Sometimes, it would take hours for the police to show up. Last night, the police arrived in less than 20 minutes, prepared to take fingerprints.

Amber told the cops she was afraid and wanted an order of protection taken out against Tyler. They advised her against it, saying it wouldn't be binding because he technically lived in a different state. The cops told Amber the best thing she could do was to move so he couldn't find her. Was she supposed to live her life in fear, running every time he found her? This type of thing was why Amber wanted to move away from her old neighborhood back home. People were constantly getting robbed or killed, or they were just going nowhere. It was as if the ghetto was keeping them where they were, constantly squashing their spirits and drives to achieve. Amber vowed long ago she would never be stuck like that. Since she was a little girl, she told herself that when she left, she was never going back. Thinking about someone breaking into her place made her angry; it was as if the ghetto followed her anyway.

First thing in the morning, Amber went down to the 7-Eleven to pick up a paper. While she was there, she picked up an apartment guide, too. She decided the first order of the day was to find herself a new place to live. Looking through the guide, she realized that finding an apartment she could afford and meet her standards at the same time was going to be more difficult than she originally thought. Amber reminded herself that she had long since quit her job. She had accepted a fellowship that would allow her to attend school full time, and it required her to only work within the school. That, combined with her breakup with Tyler, left her no choice but to drastically cut expenses. She did have the little bit of money she took from Tyler, but she planned to use that for tuition if she was accepted into a doctoral program.

Amber contemplated the decisions she was being forced to make as she opened her door to put out the trash. To her surprise, David was standing outside the door.

"Hi," David grinned at her like a Cheshire cat, like nothing at all was wrong. As soon as she saw his face, Amber knew she was not going to be angry long.

"Look what the cat dragged in. I didn't think I would be hearing from you again."

Amber contemplated all the things Che told her about David and his wife. She decided to play it cool and let him hang himself.

"What do you mean? I told you I would be busy for awhile."

Amber looked at him. She wanted to blurt out everything she knew but held back. Instead she said, "Yeah, I guess you were locked up by the old lady for being away for awhile."

David didn't answer at first.

" Oh, I see. I told you that she was gone. She went home to her mother. What happened here?"

"Never mind that!"

Amber wondered if she had the word 'fool' stamped across her forehead.   She felt her anger getting weaker.

"Really?" she said.  "I called you to let you know Tyler was in town, and a woman answered the phone.  What was that about?" David's smile vanished from his face.

"You should trust me more Amber.  You must have called the wrong number; I told you they were gone.  And so what if Big Bad Tyler was here?!  I can take care of myself!"

Amber was unsure.  Maybe she did call the wrong number. No one had answered the door.  She should know better than to listen to grapevine gossip anyway.  Although she halfway turned away from David to continue cleaning up the mess, he hugged her anyway.  Amber felt herself hugging him back.  She was relieved and started to cry again.  Through her tears she told him about the break in and that she needed to move.

"It'll be okay, just trust me."   David's deep voice became comforting.  Amber wanted to trust him but was very hesitant. She didn't want to be left sitting by the phone for another week.

"I'll tell you what."  David gently wiped away Amber's tears. "Leave all this stuff here and come and stay with me until Monday.  By then we will have found you a new place."

Amber held her breath for a second.  If she stayed with David, she could see if his wife was really gone.  That would shut Che up. But what about the neighbors?  What would they think?  They all knew her.

"How's that gonna look?  Everyone on the block knows the deal."   It would have been a good idea, but she didn't see how they could do that without people talking. David closed the door and held her tighter.

"Didn't I say to trust me? We can work all that stuff out later." Amber thought about the possibilities. Who cares what people think?! Besides, it was only for a few days.

"Okay," she said. "But only until Monday." David smiled as he held her.

"I'll help you pack," he said. Then he gave Amber a long, deep kiss. Amber kissed him back, and before long, they were making love on the floor, right in front of the door.

When she arrived at David's place, Amber walked from room to room. Although he had been inside her place when she used to live across the street, Amber never got the chance to visit David's house. He thought she was just checking it out, but she was actually looking for signs of his wife. As Amber looked around, she noticed all of David's wife's stuff was still around.

"She didn't take much", she said as she surveyed the house. David muttered something about planning to ship a lot of things to his wife.

As Amber checked out the bedroom, she noticed a charcoal drawing opposite the bed. It was a portrait of David's wife, obviously as a young girl. The way it was drawn, the eyes seemed to follow Amber around the room, watching her every move. Looking at the picture, she turned to David and asked, "Where do I sleep?"

She really wanted to know if he expected her to sleep in

another woman's bed with the woman's likeness hovering over her, watching while she screwed her husband.

David looked at Amber, then at the picture and said, "We can just take this down and put it somewhere else." That was enough to satisfy Amber, at least for the time being. "His wife must really be gone," she thought. "If she's not, he really has more balls than I thought. Even so, if he were my husband, I would definitely be kicking his ass."

David went to the restroom, and Amber walked back into the living room. She walked around, looking at the odds and ends on the curio shelf. There appeared to be what once was a bouquet of flowers on one of the shelves. They were wilted and obviously needed to be disposed of. Amber reached for the vase that the flowers were in. As she did, she noticed a card behind them on the shelf. Before she could stop herself, she was reading the inscription. "We can get through this, too. Get well soon. I love you. D."

David came up behind her, and Amber spun around, angry. She felt her face flush beet-red.

" I thought you said it was over! This is dated last week! You loved her, last week! People who are breaking up don't tell each other they love you!" David shifted his weight back and forth.

"She was in the hospital when I sent that card. What was I supposed to say? 'Die bitch, I hate your guts!' We've been together a long time, you know. We do have a son!"   As she looked at David, Amber wondered what he could have said.

Maybe she was overreacting. Her tone softened from anger to tentative sarcasm.

"What was wrong with her? Broken heart?"

David looked at Amber and sighed. "You're hard, you know that. No, she had some kind of female thing. A cyst or something. Don't worry, she's better now." He let out a breath that illustrated his annoyance.

"I don't know what I did to deserve your suspicion, but give me a break! Can we talk about something else?"

Amber stopped questioning David about his wife, but she didn't stop thinking about the situation. She couldn't believe what she was doing, but it felt good and that made it okay. Still, a tiny part of her was still feeling good old guilt. She didn't share any of the weekend's goings on with anyone, including Che. She and David had a wonderful weekend, but they didn't do much apartment hunting. Eventually, she pushed her misgivings to the back of her mind to help relieve her guilt. Things were stressful enough. David made her feel protected and that was important to her.

# 20

WHY CAN'T I HAVE *normal dreams like everyone else? I keep coming back to the same dream every night, except this time I am not in the center of the stage, but standing in the crowd with everyone else. I am even dancing with everyone else. There is a lone man in the stage tonight, he is old and bent over with age, but he is familiar even though I don't think I know him.*

*"I know you," he says. I don't answer him. I didn't speak out loud and I can't figure out how he could have possibly heard me if I did; the drumming is going on as usual and it is so loud that I am sure that people outside my dream can hear it.*

*The people are dancing and singing to the familiar rhythm and I am* moving with them, almost against my will. I can't figure it out but it is as if I know which way to move. I feel myself move and my spine undulate as if mimicking the movements of the serpent that is usually in the basket in front of me in this dream. I notice that this time the basket is in front of the old man on the stage. My grandmother is holding the basket. When did she arrive, I wonder? She looks over her shoulder and smiles at me. The lines in her face seem to have disappeared; she looks younger than I remember.

"Why do I know the steps?"

"You wrote the dance." She answers through her smile.

The people are singing around me and they are calling the old man by his name in the song as if they all know him and have known him for some time. I am the only one he is a stranger to. I watch him as he kisses the snake like I did last night and the night before that and the night before that. When I kiss the snake (or the snake kissed me), I could suddenly see, but I notice that the kiss does not have the same effect on the old guy. He kisses the snake and he drops his cane and stands up straight; he too starts to dance to the music and his whole body undulates in perfect rhythm and sync with the drums and the dancers. He knows which way to move too, never missing a beat. It is really amazing considering just a kiss ago he was bent over and his spine knotted up like old dried up driftwood.

He dances with my grandmother and she moves like a young person too. He is talking to me again and calling me to join them on the stage, but I am once again floating over my body and watching like I am watching a theatrical performance; only I am the star even though I am not, for a change, the center of the action. The crowd moves my body to dance with the old man and my grandmother and I notice he is no longer old; he is Malik. Malik is in my dream!

"What are you doing here! This is my dream!"

"You invited me, don't you remember?"

I can sense the almost-sarcasm in his voice and we dance to the rhythm while we mirror each other's movements like perfect yin and yang. The rhythm changes and gets faster, almost frantic, and I watch as I dance and I wonder why David isn't in my dream sometimes but as I dance I can still feel Malik's eyes on me. He sees into my soul just like when we are awake, only now I feel warm as I feel his eyes inside me. "He doesn't belong."

I am startled as I realize that he can hear me think.

"I can hear you louder than you hear yourself," he says, never missing a beat. I watch from overhead as we all change step with the rhythm; the dance has become almost urgent as if frenzied. We all move quickly as we sway our hips back and forth; the movements we make seem to be beckoning and playful yet mockingly sensual. The people are happy.

Even though the mood is festive, our movements are worrying me; I feel my body becoming nervous and even though I want to wake up, I watch, fascinated.

"It will be alright." Malik talks to me as he dances and smiles. "You will learn to take the good with the bad and recognize the transitions." What the hell does that mean? Dreams can be so cryptic.

*Malik falls to the ground and stops dancing. I watch as we continue our dance of death around him. No one is sad, instead they seem to rejoice as if this is the new way things are to be.*

# 21

WHEN SCHOOL STARTED Monday, Amber still had not found a new apartment. She kept telling herself it would all work out, but it was going to be a busy week. She was to start her new job as a teaching assistant; she had an interview scheduled for Friday in St. Louis at one of the graduate schools she applied to. As usual, the first day of class was hectic. No one knew where they belonged, and to top it off, Amber showed up for her first day of work and found out she inherited her first class by default! One of the professors whom Amber was to assist developed a severe medical problem the day before class began. She didn't have much time to prepare.

As she stood in front of the class, it was impossible for the students to tell that the situation was stressful at all for Amber. Her telltale paper twisting would give her away to her closest friends. Otherwise, she appeared calm. She introduced herself to the class with confidence. Looking around, she noticed the composition of the class. "It figures!" she thought. "No Black faces." She sighed and continued with the introduction of the make-shift syllabus she prepared.

After about 10 minutes, a group of late students straggled in. Obviously, these folks were not freshmen, or at least not 18-year-olds; they didn't seem the least bit frazzled about being late. Amber paused to let the latecomers take their seats. She noticed one Black student, taller than the rest in the group. He took his seat with the others, and turned and smiled at Amber.

"Oh shit!" Amber's eyes grew wide as she let the commotion die down. It was Malik from the club! He was going to be a student in her class!

After awhile, Amber regained her composure. Other than smiling across the room, Malik showed no sign of knowing her. What was he doing there? He looked a little old for freshman psychology.

Amber barely made it through the class introductions. Malik's presence was distracting. When the period was over, she dismissed the class, grateful that she made it through her first day with no significant mishaps. While gathering her things, Amber thought about the absence of Blacks on campus, and it bothered her. Education was cheap in Texas; it seemed to be more heavily subsidized by the state than it was in Louisiana. Still, people did not seem to be very education-oriented. Most of the people of color whom Amber met on campus seemed to be from somewhere else.

Amber was deep in thought as she left the classroom, so much so that she almost didn't see Malik standing by the door.

"So," he said. "Your name is Amber." His voice was so deep it took Amber by surprise. She almost dropped all of the things she carried in her arms. His diction was impeccable, but she noticed a slight southern overtone in his voice.

"Hi. Nice to see you again. I never did get a chance to tell you thanks for what you did that night," said Amber, turning to get a better view. Amber remembered meeting him that night in the club. He looked good then, but sometimes the lights in the club played tricks on the eyes.

Malik was okay looking but not handsome. He was what Che would call a "manly man". Still, he wasn't bad to look at, and he smelled good. Like that night at the club, Amber noted that he was looking really sharp. His clothes, along with his height, made him stand out from the other students milling around in the hallway.

"It was nothing," He said. "Hey, it is so nice to see a sista up there teaching. Where are you headed?"

"I am not a teacher really. I am just a TA, a graduate student. The regular professor is sick. And don't think you are gonna get over because you know me or I'm Black."

She sounded annoyed. Amber never had a Black professor herself, but if she had, she knew she wouldn't have expected handouts.

"No," he said. "I would think that means that I have to work extra hard this semester because you plan on busting my balls just for GP!" Malik grinned at Amber and she saw his gap in his teeth for the first time. She gave Malik her most phony smile.

"Whatever." She wanted him to know she meant business.

"I ain't about all that, Africa. I'm here to get an education!" He began to walk with her. "I'm new on campus, and I still don't quite know where things are. Can you tell me where the cafeteria is? Better, yet, do you plan on eating lunch?"

Amber looked at Malik. Everyone was always trying to get over, one way or another, but he was such a gentleman the other week in the club that he had to be harmless. Maybe she was being a little hard on him. There was no crime in showing him the way.

"I wasn't really planning on eating, but I'll show you where the cafeteria is. It's on the other side of campus, a little hard to find your first time."

Malik accompanied Amber to her office so she could drop her books, then they made their way to the student union, where the cafeteria was housed. Amber liked to check out what was happening in the union, although it was the hangout for undergrads. As a graduate student, she didn't participate in many of the activities, but it was still fun to go and people watch. The campus was so big the only place Black students who weren't athletes ran into each other was in the union.

Amber ended up staying and having lunch with Malik. Although she thought she wasn't hungry, her stomach growled as soon as she smelled food. Throughout lunch, the conversation stayed very light and Malik continued to be cordial. They discussed the school and its various programs. Malik told Amber he was a freshman. He went into the military to get money for college and was planning to use the GI Bill to finance his education. Amber sat with Malik in the student union until almost 1:30p.m. Then she remembered that David was supposed to pick her up at 2:00p.m. back at her office. She glanced at her watch and stood up.

"I almost forgot, I gotta run!"

"So soon? He can wait!"

Malik grabbed Amber's sleeve and smiled. Perplexed, she looked down at him still sitting at the table. How did he know she was meeting someone? After a minute, Amber realized he didn't actually know, he couldn't. He was kidding her.

"I've got an appointment. See you in class!" Amber tried to walk away again, and as she did Malik added, "Maybe we can get together."

She should have known. Everybody wanted something. She wiped the smile off of her face.

"Look, Malik. You're cool and all, but I am going to be your lecturer this semester. I think it would be best if we keep our relationship on the professional level. It'll make things easier for both of us, especially when I have to fail you."

It was her turn to smile. Malik let go of her arm, handed her a card.

"Dang, woman! I wasn't asking to get married, just keep in touch! I don't know a lot of folks around here. Here's my number."

Amber stuffed the number into her pocket as she quickly walked away, feeling a twinge of guilt for being so snippy. It passed quickly; she didn't want to keep David waiting. They were supposed to spend the afternoon finding her new apartment. She wanted to be moved in before she left for her interview on Friday.

Amber reached her office just as David drove up. As soon as she saw him, Amber smiled.

Amber hopped into David's car, and they headed away from campus.

"I have a surprise for you." David was grinning from ear to ear. "I played hookie from work today."

After it became obvious that David had no intentions of telling what was up his sleeve, Amber changed the subject.

"Guess what? I am going to <u>teach</u> a class, not assist. And guess what else? I actually have a Black student."

David looked at her, but didn't answer. He was waiting for more information. The uniqueness of the situation was lost on him. As Amber began to explain the racial composition of the campus to David, they pulled into a parking lot. Cutting her off,

David turned to her and handed her a set of keys.

"Here. These are for you." Amber was confused as he walked her to a ground floor apartment.

David talked, explaining himself as they walked from room to room. "I took the liberty of saving you the trouble of looking and did it for you. I thought this might be your kind of place."

Amber looked around, and he was right, it was. The apartment was four times the size of her old one. It had two of everything: two bedrooms, two baths and two parking spaces. To top it off, David had moved most of her things into the apartment already.

"You sure were counting on me liking it." Amber looked around with mixed feelings. She did like the apartment, but she was sort of looking forward to doing the looking herself.

"David, I can't afford this." Amber knew he meant well, but as her eyes browsed around the apartment she knew he was unaware of her budget.

"Trust me, I took care of everything." As he spoke, he showed her copies of the leasing agreement. He put everything in his name, including the utilities.

Amber paused a minute. Why did she feel uneasy every time he said "trust me"?

"You don't have to worry about anything. Just concentrate on getting into that graduate school you want so much!"

Amber wished it were as easy as he made it seem. It was just as well. She never imagined herself a kept woman, but since he was willing to invest the money, why not? She would try anything once, as long as no one knew.

"I'll catch up to you later. Get acclimated. I have some things to do. I need to take my car to get worked on."

David prepared to leave, and as he did, he asked Amber if she could pick him up at the car repair shop later that afternoon. Amber agreed to meet him in a couple of hours, and perhaps go to dinner. It was the least she could do. He did save her a lot of time and trouble, and she needed to work on her first real lecture.

As she unpacked her things, Amber realized she hadn't spoken with Che in a couple of days. She looked around, noticing how neatly David moved her things; he helped her pack the night before. He seemed so carefree, yet everything was uncharacteristically organized and in its place. Her phone was even plugged in. Amber picked it up and there was a dial tone. How had he gotten the phone turned on so fast?

She dialed Che's number and immediately told her about her new place, leaving out the David details.

"So you're moving on up, huh woman? That's a pretty nice area, much nicer than before. I'm surprised they let you in!" Amber couldn't tell whether she was pessimistic or jealous. Che could never be happy for her, but Amber was in a good mood and she planned to stay there. There was no way she was going to fight with Che today. Rather than be annoyed, Amber acted as if her call waiting was beeping in. She smirked to herself, she didn't even know if David installed call waiting as an option. Since Che was being funky, Amber created an excuse to hang up.

"Oop, gotta go, girlie. Someone's calling. I check ya later."

"Yeah, well, I understand, you are the society woman now. Give me a call if you feel like slummin'."

Amber hung up and called her voice messaging service at her old number. As she punched in her code, she reminded herself, in advance, to call the phone company and get the old number disconnected. To her surprise, there was a message from her father. Usually, they spoke to each other every Sunday, and this was Monday. Speaking with her dad was like going to church; she felt it was the way to start the week out right. Her father was not fond of long distance telephoning, and to keep the telephone bills down, they rarely called each other during the week.

Amber dialed her father's number in Louisiana and as soon as he picked up, she asked, "What's wrong?" She felt a sense of doom. Her dad was usually concerned with "using up his phone", so his weekday call could only mean trouble.

"Bout time you called," he said gruffly. "I coulda been dead or something, and you would have never known." Same old dad. He definitely had a flair for the melodramatic. Amber anticipated his next question.

"When you coming home? I don't like you being so far away." Amber sighed; it was always the same, even when she and Tyler were together. He wanted her home, preferably without Tyler. He couldn't understand why she had no desire to live in the old neighborhood.

"Let's not go there again Dad. What's up?" His voice softened and he explained to Amber that her college friend, LaShaun, had died over the weekend. LaShaun was shot at a neighborhood house party. Amber was silent.

"Damn! Another one." She knew several people who had died the same way. "Why are people shooting each other?"

"The funeral is three days away. I can send you a ticket."

"No, Dad, you can't. We can't afford it, so I can't come."

"LaShaun was your friend!"

"So I know she would understand. Go for me, Dad. Give her mother my condolences." He grunted instead of answering her.

Amber and LaShaun got to be good friends during college. LaShaun transferred into the school the year after Amber graduated and wanted to become a cheerleader. It was her fourth college, and her fourth cheerleading team, so she was very good at it. Amber became the cheerleading coach that same year. LaShaun was a year older than Amber was, and at the time they seemed to have a lot in common. They became close and stayed that way until Amber got married and left Louisiana. Although they kept in touch after Amber left, over time they drifted apart. As they got older, they seemed to "grow up" differently or something.

Now Amber was working on her graduate degree, and LaShaun was still in college. When they met, LaShaun was a transfer student from the neighboring college in the next parish; it seemed like she was in college for ten years. The last time

Amber had gone home to visit, she noticed that LaShaun had developed a "street edge" to her. She took Amber to a neighborhood hole in the wall that was trying to pass for a club; Amber never knew the place existed. Amber was perturbed the whole evening; it just wasn't her type of place. She was so busy being sophisticated that she blamed their now obvious differences on LaShaun. She told herself LaShaun had changed.

Remembering the incident, she realized that maybe she was the one who had done the changing. Back in college, she and LaShaun had frequented those kinds of places often, and she never gave two thoughts about it. She had grown up, and lost her "street edge" that Louisiana had given her. LaShaun said Amber had become a woman of the world. LaShaun had only been outside of Louisiana twice, both were attempts to attend two different colleges. Both times she came back home as fast as she could.

Amber now thought about how she acted with LaShaun that night. She was so funky with her friend. She knew LaShaun had probably called her "hincty" under her breath. Amber could hear her saying that word as plain as day. She was gone now though. Amber felt sorry for her.

As she continued sifting through her things, Amber realized she probably wasn't as sad as she should be. It was as if a stranger had died rather than someone who was once her running buddy.

"Damn, girl, you hard!" She imagined David talking to her as she looked down at her watch. As she did, she remembered their appointment. Where did the time go? It was time for her to meet David. She picked up her bag and headed out the door.

# 22

"SHIT!"

Amber looked at her watch. David was supposed to pick her up 20 minutes ago. When his car first went into the shop, Amber chauffeured him wherever he needed to go. By the end of the week, he was pretty much driving her car all the time, taking Amber back and forth to campus. She had let him use her car to go to work, with the agreement that he would meet her and take her to the airport in time for her flight. She was leaving town for her interview in St. Louis.

Amber had not heard from David since the morning, and she was beginning to get worried. It was obvious he had no intention of showing up. She had confirmed she would be at her interview at the last minute and didn't want to reschedule. Watching the time, she called Che; maybe she could take her to the airport.

She knew Che was going to give her a hard time, but she was going to have to bite the bullet. Che chewed on her ear all week about letting David drive her car.

"Girl, if David has as much money as he would have you think, why can't he rent a car?"

"Why should he have to rent?" she replied. "That's wasteful. I am just giving him a hand keeping what he got! Mind your own business anyway!"

"Why should you help him keep anything?! It ain't like he spends it on you, is it?"

Amber thought about the long diatribe of "I told you so's" she was going to have to deal with from Che and opted to take a car service to the airport. As she dialed the number, she thought about how much the 40-minute ride would set her back financially. David was saving money and she was spending it. Wasn't he the one with the real job? Her airline ticket was expensive, and she knew she really could not afford it. Although her job as a teaching assistant provided her with some funds, she was by no means rolling in the dough. Her salary was not luxurious; it provided just enough money to barely cover the basics.

Amber's car arrived and as she rode to the airport she thought about David and couldn't believe the way she was letting herself be jerked around. How dare he not show up! Something obviously must be wrong or he would have been there. At least he would have called. She hoped the "something" had nothing to do with her car.

You gotta do what you gotta do. There was no way she intended on missing this interview; it was very important to her. Not all applicants get asked to an interview. Amber knew the invitation meant she had obviously made it to the final round of the application process. Knowing this, she spent weeks preparing, not confirming the interview until she was sure she was as prepared as she possibly could be. She researched the school and its programs as well as the professors. She even looked up the interests of the faculty; Amber made sure she at least knew what the last publication of each faculty member was about. She was prepared to discuss these somewhat intelligently. She would worry about David and her car later.

Amber paid the taxi fare; the ill-planned trip to the airport cost her $40.

"Wait until I catch up to David," she thought as she walked into the airport. "If he couldn't be around, I could have made other plans." Amber fumed when she realized airport parking for the weekend would have been cheaper than taking the taxi.

Her flight was scheduled to leave in 20 minutes. When she approached the gate, passengers were already boarding. Still, she quickly ducked into a newsstand to grab a magazine. As she left the newsstand, she noticed David running toward her.

"Amber, wait!" The sight of David made her angrier.

"How fucking nice of you to show up! If I had waited for you, I might have missed my plane!"

"Time got away from me, I was playing basketball and lost track of the time." David hung his head and looked up at her with his best puppy-dog eyes.

"Lost track of the time! You wanted me to miss my plane! You just make sure you take care of my car for the weekend!"

Amber turned and walked away. She was afraid that if she kept talking, she would either cry or slap David. She felt the tears welling up in her eyes anyway; she could feel them blurring her vision as she tried to make her way to her seat on the plane. They made a lump in her throat and she swallowed hard, trying to focus her thoughts on her upcoming interview. She pulled out her notes and began to review answers to questions most likely to be asked.

When she arrived in St. Louis, she checked into her motel near the college. The college had recommended it to her because of its proximity to the campus. The motel was small and smelled old and historic. It looked like it could be part of the campus itself.

After her interview, Amber was scheduled to spend time with the program's current students. The other students were supposed to show her around and tell her how great things were for them since they had chosen to get a graduate degree in industrial psychology. Amber guessed that she had been paired with the graduate school's other 'token' minority, and was right. Throughout the whole weekend she saw only one other Black student. Overall, she was not impressed. Even the professors in her interview seemed to be on edge about the lack of minority students.

David left several messages for Amber at her motel, but she didn't return any of his calls. When she returned to her room, it was usually too late to call him back.

She went to dinner with the other students the second night. She also took a tour of the campus, which took her mind off of her problems back home in Austin. Before Amber knew it, Sunday morning arrived, and it was time for her to return home to Austin.

She half expected David not to meet her at the airport. Not only was he there, but he arrived with flowers.

David was grinning ear to ear. Amber looked at his grin and once again, she knew she wasn't going to stay mad at him. Every time he smiled like that, her stomach flip-flopped.

"You must have known you were in the dog house."

Without answering, David gave Amber a long hug and handed her the flowers.

"I missed you so much. Next time I'm going with you."
Amber laughed. "Business is business, baby. You weren't invited. I couldn'ta concentrated with you there."

He was extremely sweet to Amber on the way back to her apartment. He opened her car door and kept smiling at her during the ride. They stopped for lunch at Amber's favorite restaurant.

"So, why were you avoiding me all weekend? Why didn't you return my calls?" David asked. "How many guys hit on you, baby?"

"So that's it. I thought you really missed me. The real deal is you think I met someone else and would leave or something!"

Amber looked at David across the table as he refilled her wineglass. She sucked her teeth. He was smiling at her but Amber could sense the seriousness in his conversation. He was really jealous at the possibility of her meeting someone else.

"When I am ready to leave, I will let you know. You just make sure you don't pull anymore stunts like the one you did with my car."

Instead of giving him the information he wanted, Amber decided to leave him guessing, maybe he would stay on his toes.

They went back to her place after lunch. Amber noticed David had taken the liberty of putting some of his things in the closet and around the apartment during the weekend.

"Oh, so you just think because you found this place you can just move on up in here, huh?"

She tried to be serious, but it was hard to keep from smiling. It was obvious David was doing what women did when they were trying to mark their territory. He wanted any other man who might come there to see that a man was around.

"It's not like that. I thought it would be easier to just leave a couple of things here."

He had a sheepish grin on his face. He hugged Amber from behind as he spoke, kissing her on her neck.

"Let me show you how much I missed you."

By letting David kiss her, Amber realized she missed him too. She felt herself begin to react to him physically. David had the ability to arouse her with a touch; something Tyler never accomplished.

"Are we going to the gym in the morning?" she asked as he undressed her.

"Nope, we are going to be doing our workout right here!"

"You know that's corny, right?" Amber laughed as she thought about how corny he was: corny and charming.

David began to unbutton her jeans. He could charm the panties off her every time. He led her into the bedroom; Amber let him do as he pleased. She wasn't mad anymore, but Amber had not forgotten about David not showing up with her car. They would discuss the new ground rules for her car later.

# 23

"SO. DID DAVID MISS YOU while you were out of town or what?" Che could not resist bringing up David when she and Amber met at McDonald's for lunch

"Yup. He sure did. Don't you worry, I got me some as soon as I got in. David met me at the airport, and we made up for the whole weekend." Amber smirked. She could hear Che draw in her breath.

"Speaking of David, did you let him have your car for the weekend? You know, I saw him all over town. I can't believe you would let him drive like that. You know he probably had other women up in there!"

Amber knew before she even got a chance to talk with Che she had nothing but negative stuff to say about the situation.

"Didn't anyone ever tell you that if you have nothing good to say you shouldn't say anything at all? As a matter of fact, from now on, don't tell me anything about David! Just do us both a favor and keep whatever it is to yourself!" Amber snapped at Che. She refused to let Che stir up dirt, even if stirring dirt was Che's favorite pastime.

"Touchy, touchy. You have been so defensive lately. Whatever happened to friends are friends for life, with men being expendable?" Che could sense she was getting to Amber; she liked it.

"You seem to be more concerned with your relationship with David than you are with our friendship. Is the dick that good, girl?"

"Tcchh!" Amber sucked her teeth. She was annoyed and Che could not resist pushing her just a little further.

"You know I could make you feel as good, if not better than he can, but you won't give me a chance!"

Since she was sticking pins in soft spots, she may as well try them all. Che laughed to herself,

"Why do we have to go there?" Amber was just short of yelling. "From now on, both of those subjects are closed, or we can't be friends! Besides, that stupid saying is your motto, not mine!"

She didn't feel up to Che's games and wanted to end the

conversation. Che was surprised Amber was raising her voice. Usually, she would be more concerned with what people thought around her.

"Fine. No problem. But don't come running to me when he fucks you over, and you know he will. From what I hear, he did it to his wife, and he will do it to you too. Enjoy it while it lasts!"

Amber sucked in her breath at Che's remarks. Che sure knew how to set her off, but she damn sure didn't want her to know how much. She couldn't let Che get the best of her, not today.

She paused and she imagined herself spitting in Che's face. She counted to ten and watched the saliva in slow motion, flying across the restaurant table and landing right below Che's left eye. The table was small enough; she could probably hit her mark; target spitting was one of the more unattractive things she had learned from her father. She passed on some of the more colorful insults that she also had learned from her father, instead mumbling a low, "Whatever, Che. You are always in my business."

"What the hell does that mean?!" Che paused. "Girl, You ain't right and you know it. You talk about me!"

Amber's remark was enough to relieve most of the tension that was building between them. They looked at each other and broke into a laugh. Other people in the restaurant turned to look at them. They laughed almost to the point of tears. Che knew she had pushed Amber far enough. From that point in their conversation, neither mentioned David, and the conversation became light. Amber told Che about her interview, but she could tell from the way Che kept looking around she wasn't really interested.

When Amber got back to her car, she noticed a piece of paper on her windshield. It was stuck underneath her wiper blades. She hated flyers on her car. What kind of a person took a job doing windshield advertising anyway?

Amber grabbed the paper and threw it on the seat next to her while she waved good-bye to Che. She didn't give the flyer another thought as she headed toward school. Her mind was still on the conversation between her and Che.

Amber could tell Che definitely had a problem with her relationship with David. She couldn't figure out if Che was being protective or if she was jealous. Above all, Che was needy. She needed Amber's attention and friendship and resented the time Amber was spending with David.

She wondered about her knack for attracting needy friends. This wasn't the first time she had a friend like Che. Many of her friends seemed to have had some type of emotional dependence on her. What did that say about her? Did she have some deep-seated need for people to depend on her or something? Her relationship with Che was a problem. In a way, she knew she needed Che, too.

Although Che was sometimes a pain in the ass, in some ways, she made Amber feel good about herself, more like she had it together. Seeing Che's shortcomings made Amber feel good, and she realized that many of the mean things Che said and did were rooted in jealousy. She hated to admit this to herself, but it was the jealousy that made her feel good, even confident. It was just what she needed when she was feeling insecure.

Recently, Amber felt more insecure than ever before. She needed Che around for validation that she still had it. Her life was uprooted; she and Tyler had really split. It was almost unbelievable. When she was with him, she had never felt insecure. She knew all about him and could practically tell him what he would be thinking next. Amber never imagined they would be apart. With David, she wasn't sure how long or if he would be around. He was so good looking; lots of people were interested in him. He could be gone tomorrow. And he was always lying about something or embellishing the ordinary.

Amber remembered Tyler watching his talk shows. She had told Tyler that he was just watching them to make himself feel better about what was happening in his life. Similar to how Che's jealousy made her feel better about herself.

"Whatever." She said aloud in her car as she pulled up in the university parking lot. Every relationship has its purpose.

"She's using me, and I'm using her. We'll just call it a symbiotic relationship. We're like parasites."

Amber picked up her things from her car seat and glanced at the paper she had taken from her windshield. She noticed a note written on the back: "David, give me a call when you get a chance. Linda."

Who in the hell was Linda? Why was she leaving a note for David on her car? Amber's first instinct was to drive to wherever David was and ask him about this Linda, but she had no idea where David was. Amber looked at the note again. She wondered if Che was right all along. Was David really driving women around in her car all weekend? And this Linda sure had some nerve. Even if David did have someone in the car, it should have been obvious the car belonged to a woman. Amber had taken her name off the front of her car after the stalking incident, but her sorority license plate frame was still on the front: Alpha Kappa Alpha, in big pink letters. The pink color clashed with the red exterior of her car; it could be spotted from across the street. Couldn't be missed. She also had an air freshener hanging from her rear view mirror with AKA on it. At least the air freshener hung there until she let David drive her car. After the first time it had torn; David claimed that he had left the window open on the car and the wind was so strong it had torn the air freshener down. Amber realized she had the same air freshener hanging in her window for quite awhile, and it had never torn before.

"It's January."

Why would he drive with the window down in January anyway? This year had been unusually cool. Maybe Che was right, maybe he was macking in her car. He probably took the air freshener down on purpose. He might have taken the license plate off too.

"What an asshole! Does he think I am stupid or what?"

Amber looked at her watch again. She was going to be late for class. She would obviously have to deal with David later.

Amber had a hard time concentrating in class. She spent most of the three hours thinking about David and trying to figure out what it was he had actually done and who he had done it with while she was out of town. She thought about the time they had spent together when she returned from St. Louis. She couldn't help wondering if he was really happy to see her or if all the attention was due to his guilty conscience. What if Che was right? What if David really was just trying to play her for a fool?

Hearing her instructor dismissing class, Amber realized she had not heard a word of the lecture or taken so much as a single line of notes. She stood up and closed her books, noticing her doodling in the notebook margins. It was unlike her to let things get her so distracted. Even when she and Tyler were having problems, she was able to just block everything out while she was in class. She usually pushed whatever was bothering her to the back of her mind and focused on the things the instructor was saying.

Amber headed for the graduate office around the corner from the lecture hall. From down the hallway, she could see someone waiting outside her door. As she got closer, she recognized Malik.

She didn't try very hard to mask her annoyance at his intrusion; she rolled her eyes and frowned. She needed to prepare for her lecture and did not have time to socialize. She didn't even say hello even though he was smiling at her.

"What is it, Malik?  I'm kinda busy." She snapped, causing the smile to fade from his face.

"A hello would be nice.  I just came by to let you know I won't be in class tomorrow. Can you tell me what I should read?" Amber was immediately embarrassed.

"Look, I'm sorry.  Come on in, I can tell you what the class will be about."

Malik followed Amber into her office and sat by her desk. Amber gave him a copy of her lecture outline, but he didn't leave. He sat back in the chair near her desk and began talking about the past week and weekend.

"What have you been up to, Amber?"

"Well, I moved into a new place."

Amber's eyes lit up with excitement.  She leaned to the side and placed her hands on her hip.  Her tone became friendlier as she told Malik about her new apartment.  When she told him the name of the complex, he looked surprised.

"No kidding?  Then we are neighbors.  I live there too, in apartment 531."

Amber raised her eyebrows.  She was just as surprised a Malik. He lived right on the other side of the same apartment complex. Malik continued.  "I didn't know they let more than one of us live there!"

"Yeah," Malik added.  "Up to now I think I was the only one. So, how was your interview?"

Amber had told Malik she would be going out of town to St.

Louis for an interview, and he remembered.

"It was very nice. Thanks. I probably won't hear anything until April 15."

Amber explained how that was the date most schools announced their decisions. To her surprise, Malik appeared genuinely interested.

"I don't think it's the place for me anyway. It was kinda cold. I didn't feel welcome."

"You probably did fine anyway, Amber. Maybe we could go hang out to celebrate. Better yet, maybe you should come over, and I can make you dinner to celebrate."

Amber didn't want to give Malik the wrong idea. With all the man-trouble she was having, she didn't feel like making her life any more complicated.

"Thanks, but I don't think that's such a good idea."

She left out the part about her and David.

"Look, Africa, we are neighbors now. Besides, if I remember correctly, you owe me one."

Amber remembered the note on her car. Malik was right, she did owe him one. She didn't owe David anything. It was probably best to keep her options open, David obviously was. Besides, it might not hurt to have a friendly neighbor.

"Let me think about it." Amber smiled at Malik. At least she wasn't saying no. At least she knew <u>he</u> wasn't married. Malik stood up to leave.

"Fine. At least you'll think about it. I just want to be

neighborly. Let me know by the weekend, here's my number. Maybe we can plan something."

He wrote his number on a Post-It note and dropped it on her desk. Before Amber could answer, he had turned, and walked out of the door and down the hall.

# 24

AMBER WAS ACTUALLY going out with David. For the first time, she was not going out to meet him somewhere, but actually going out with him on a date. Two days after Amber had found the note on her car, they had patched up their differences. He had explained to Amber that the note from Linda was innocent-- she was a co-worker. She saw the car in McDonald's and thought it was his. The phone system in the office was being upgraded and since she had wanted to talk with him about a big presentation for his boss the following week, she thought a note on the car might be a way to get in touch with him.

"I have no idea why she left that note on your car," he

explained with a straight face. "Maybe she saw me driving it and just thought it belonged to me."

Amber wanted to believe him; she couldn't resist his charm and his smile. The sexual chemistry between them made her forget everything, including how angry she was with him. He swore it would never happen again and to make it up to her, he promised to take her to the club.

As Amber got ready to go out, she thought about Che and the surprised look she would have on her face when she and David showed up together. Che never had anything good to say about David. Since their conversation in McDonald's, she didn't mention him at all. Amber could sense her shock over the phone when she broke the news that she would not be riding with her.

"I'll meet you there," Amber had told her.

"Meet me there? We always ride together!"

"Look, I will just talk to you later."

Amber knew Che was curious as hell, and Amber loved it.

She planned to make a grand entrance at the club. She had made a special shopping trip for the occasion, the result was a tight fitting, white leather dress. It was cut just low enough to be sexy but still left something to the imagination. Amber had purchased the dress because it made her "B" cups look more like a pair of "C's". She usually passed on the low-cut dresses because she felt her chest was too small. Che, who was very well endowed in the chest area, often joked about her need for a Miracle bra. Even though she had laughed with Che, it was a sore spot for her.

As she watched her reflection in the mirror, she smiled, jutting her breasts out more. "I finally got me some cleavage!"

Since their "discussion" about her car, David was on his "P's" and "Q's". He was putting forth extra effort to make sure Amber was happy. He was on time for every meeting they had scheduled and was extra sweet. He even volunteered to replace Amber's electronic organizer book, which Amber couldn't find since she moved into her new apartment. Although he couldn't possibly replace the information that had been lost with the electronic organizer book, Amber still thought his offer was thoughtful. She couldn't imagine where her electronic phone book had gotten to. She wanted a new one anyway, but the new versions cost more than she could afford.

Because David was on such good behavior, she didn't hound him about his wife, either. Apparently she was really gone; David was spending more and more time with Amber. She didn't bring it up, and he didn't volunteer any more information, so they just didn't talk about it. Her impending divorce and David's supposed breakup with his wife were subjects they just didn't talk about. David made her feel so good, she kinda thought that if they didn't talk about them, then the unpleasant situations would just work themselves out.

Things were going well for Amber this week, and she was in good spirits as a result. She still hadn't heard from Tyler. He didn't know how to reach her directly, his lawyer could call hers if he had something to say. He didn't call her family. No one had seen him in town since the weekend she went skiing. Obviously, his new job and life were working out. Amber was sure that if they weren't, she probably would have heard from him. Although her feelings were still bruised, Amber wasn't going to let him or anyone else know how she felt.

Amber was putting the final touches on her lipstick as the doorbell rang. David was right on time. When they got to the club, Che was there, just as Amber planned. To Amber's surprise, Che was standing by the bar talking to none other than Malik! What a shame that was; he seemed like such a nice guy. Amber hoped he wasn't falling for Che's line. She could be such a dog!

Amber and David made their way over to the bar, near Che and Malik.

"Hey, girl, what's up!"

Amber put on her best smile to greet her friend.

"Oh, hey Malik. I didn't know you would be here."

She flashed her eyes at him as he checked her out. Malik leaned past David to give Amber a hug.

"Well, aren't you full of surprises, Amber. Or should I call you Miss LaReaux?"

Amber noticed his accent made her name sound like two separate words. It sounded more like "La Rew" than the way it was supposed to.

"Girl, you didn't tell me Mr. Malik was in your class!"

Che was tipsy, talking louder than necessary. David cleared

his throat.

"She didn't tell me either." David was annoyed. "By the way, my name is David. What's up man?" He reached over to shake Malik's hand. Amber didn't notice the puzzled look on Malik's face, or the momentary pause before he reached his hand out to shake David's.

"Yeah, what's up." Malik looked from Amber to David as their hands met.

At that moment, Che grabbed Malik's hand, leading him toward the dance floor.

"If I remember correctly, you're a pretty good dancer. Let's go!"

Malik looked back at Amber but followed Che anyway. Amber watched as they pushed through the crowd, making their way to an open spot.

"You didn't tell me about him."

Amber turned to David, noticing his annoyance.

"I didn't realize I was supposed to. Besides, I tried to, the day you surprised me with the apartment but obviously you weren't listening. What are you, jealous?" She knew David would never admit to jealousy.

A tall girl interrupted their conversation, wearing a dress so tight it forced her to take very small steps. She walked up to the bar, placing herself between Amber and David. Amber noted that she was reed thin, without hips and at least six feet tall.

"Hey, David, how ya been?"

Her voice was saccharin-sweet. Her closeness to David made Amber uncomfortable. David returned her warm welcome with a hug while she ordered a drink. David made no moves to introduce the girl, until she put her hand on his shoulder. Amber cleared her throat and extended her hand for a handshake. She did not attempt to hide her annoyance in her voice; she hissed as she spoke.

"Oh, excuse me, I don't think we've met!" Amber looked David in the eye, and he looked uncomfortable, shuffling his weight from foot to foot.

"Uh, Amber...." It was too late.

"You didn't tell me you were here with anyone, David," said the girl. She was glaring and made no attempt to shake Amber's hand.

"Ebony, this is my friend, Amber."

Amber noticed the underarm ring appearing on his shirt as David started to sweat. He moved closer to her and put his arm around her shoulder, as if he was trying to make up for slighting her in the beginning. Amber smiled sarcastically at Ebony, who stepped back from the bar when her drink arrived.

"I'll catch you later David, when you are less occupied." Ebony walked away, with both David and Amber looking on.

Amber turned back to David, pissed off.

"Less occupied?! What was that supposed to mean?"

Amber placed her hand on her hip as she referred to Ebony's tall stature. "And am I just a friend now? I didn't know you liked the Olive Oyl type."

She was hissing at David, who had a look on his face similar to that of a kid who just got caught with his hand in the cookie jar.

"So, where do you know Miss Ebony, or should we say Miss Charcoal from?"

"Just because someone is dark-skinned doesn't mean she is a bad person."

David spoke in a too-cool voice, without looking at her. Instead, he surveyed the dance floor. Amber noticed he was sidestepping the question and was not about to let him get away with it.

"Excuse me, but I don't believe that's what I asked you, David."

She stepped around, again moving into David's line of vision.

To her surprise, David grabbed her by the arm.

"Stop jumping to conclusions! Look, you obviously don't tell me everything, and I forgot to share some things with you. You don't ask me any questions, and I won't ask you any questions about Mr. Malik either! Deal!?"

Amber, surprised at David's outburst, looked around as he spoke to her. Hopefully no one noticed his vice grip on her arm. He was holding her so tight she was sure he was going to leave palm prints on her arm. No one had spoken to her in that manner or treated her like that since she and Tyler had their infamous fight. Her anger at David gave way to hurt and humiliation. She pulled her arm from his grip and spat back at him.

"Malik? Malik is different than Ms. Thing! He's just a student. Besides, I introduced you to him and he wasn't pawing all over me in front of you!"

Amber felt the tears well up in her eyes as she stepped away from David, who was still angry. She realized she and David were having their first fight and wished it didn't have to be in a public place, especially here, in the club.

"I wouldn't say he was any different. At least not by the way he was checking you out when we walked up!"

Amber tried to turn away from David, with the sound of his voice bringing on more tears. Her tears were too much for him. As the teardrops welled up in her eyes, David's face softened. He stepped toward her, drawing her closer.

"I'm sorry, Amber," he said softly. "Don't cry, I didn't mean to upset you." Amber moved closer to him. "We didn't come here to fight, let's try and have a good time. We can talk about this all later, okay?"

David looked in her eyes as he cupped Amber's chin in his hand. He kissed her on her forehead, and Amber once again felt her anger and hurt disappearing.

David took Amber's hand. "You know what? We should be dancing anyway. Let's go." Amber shook her head as he led her toward the dance floor. Their argument was forgotten as they danced together and for the first time Amber didn't feel guilty about it. They danced for several songs until Amber noticed Che and Malik from the corner of her eye. They were dancing together and apparently having a good time. Che was laughing and even from the distance, appeared tipsy. Without looking obvious, Amber danced David backward until they were dancing next to Malik and Che.

Amber smiled over at them.

"Hey, folks!"

She leaned over so Che could hear her.

"Whew, girl! This song is definitely the jam, ain't it?"

The four continued to dance, moving back and forth to the music. Amber looked out of the corner of her eye, trying to figure out if anything was going on between Che and Malik.

"I think I am about ready to get out of here." Che talked while making leaving motions with her head. She continued to smile at both Amber and Malik.

"I hope you don't plan on letting your girl drive home alone in her condition, Amber."

David seemed suddenly concerned. Amber looked from Malik to Che. She believed Che was much more sober than she was letting on.

"Well, we can always call her a cab!"

Amber watched as Che spun around in circles, supposedly dancing to the music.

"You know, she can leave her car here. I'll drive her home." Malik shrugged his shoulders. "I don't mind. Really."

Malik was back to being the gentlemen. Amber narrowed her eyes. What the hell was Che up to? She screwed Malik's friend last time, now she was after him, too?

"You don't have to do that, Malik. We have been here before, if you know what I mean. She'll be fine in a cab." Amber noticed Che frown at her slightly.

"No, we wouldn't send you home alone in a cab. I think Malik taking her home is a good idea," David said. "Better yet, Amber, you could drive her car home for her."

Amber watched as Che let Malik lead her away, as if she were as helpless as Penelope Pitstop tied to a railroad track. Damn! Did she have to sleep with everything, especially when that "everything" was someone she had to face almost everyday? Amber was miffed at the idea of Malik and Che together, but continued to dance with David. She didn't want to seem too preoccupied with her friend and her business. It wasn't all Che's fault, she thought to herself. Malik was a grown man and should be able to sense what was going on. Obviously, he had as big a part in the whole thing as did Che; Amber guessed the "dog" she knew was in Che was in Malik too. He was going to show his true colors. The southern gentleman thing was a facade. Che might not be as affected by alcohol as she pretended to be, but she was still tipsy, and apparently Malik intended to take advantage of that.

"Your boy is trying to get it on, huh?" David smirked at Amber. By now they had stopped dancing and were standing on the side of the dance floor. Maybe it just wasn't Amber's night.

"Whaddya mean by that, David? Not everybody is like you, you know?"

"Look, I'm not saying everybody is like me, but a man is a man! What do you care? Jealous?" Turnabout was definitely fair play. Hadn't she just asked him the same question?

"No, I'm not jealous. Why would I be? Look, I think it's time we call it a night." Amber was definitely not enjoying this. She planned to have a great time, and it was not turning out that way.

Amber passed on answering David's question. "Can we go?" she said, annoyed.

"Are we leaving together?" David looked at Amber.

"Are you asking me if you can come to my place?" She didn't wait for an answer. "No, I don't think so. I am kinda tired. I'll be alright." Besides, she felt like being alone.

Amber smiled and kissed him on the cheek, noticing the disappointment written all over his face.

David walked her out to the parking lot, where she had to search for Che's car. Che and Malik had obviously left some time ago, Amber noted, without even saying good-bye. As Amber drove home alone, she thought of the two of them and what they might be doing.

"I thought he might be different," she said out loud, referring to Malik. "Guess I was wrong."

As she thought about it, she felt foolish. "Guess I gotta strike that one off my list!" Amber laughed to herself. Maybe she was as bad as Che. As least Che's intentions were obvious. Amber realized she had planned to keep Malik around in case her relationship with David went sour. She was, so to speak, not putting all her eggs in one basket. She also pushed David away, she realized, because she was angry with him and jealous of his friend, Ebony.

# 25

"YOU NEVER TOLD ME about Malik! Girl, he is fine!" Che had a good time at the club, and she wanted to rub it in.

"So, did you two hit it off, or what?" Usually, it didn't take much prompting for Che to tell Amber about her escapades, but this time she was playing hard to get. Amber was dying to know what had happened between Malik and Che.

"Oh, girl, you know he is such a gentlemen. He took me home and tucked me in. Thanks for dropping my car off last night." Che was not about to give up any information. She wanted to make Amber squirm, like she often did to her. Besides, why was Amber suddenly so interested in Malik? She usually didn't want to hear what happened, or at least she acted that way.

"What was up wit you and lover-boy? He finally decided to come out of hiding and be seen with you in public, huh?" Che was trying to change the subject. She wanted the spotlight to be on Amber, not her.

"Weren't you having a good time? It looked like you were arguing." Che noticed Amber seemed annoyed all night.

Amber didn't particularly want to give Che anything new to talk about, but she felt as if she needed to talk to someone.

"Well, I wasn't really upset, but some heifer came over and was all over him, girl. He didn't even bother to introduce us, until I said something. Even then I had to twist his arm." Che listened intently.

"Girl, I told you he was no good. He don't have no respect for you." Che still hadn't told Amber about her encounter with David, and she didn't intend to. She knew by the way David had started to respond to her that he was eventually going to hurt her friend. When he did, Amber would come to her.

"I don't know what the deal is, " Amber replied. "I just had to put him in his place!" They laughed. "At any rate, we patched it up, and he is taking me out again tonight. We're supposed to meet for dinner."

After Amber had refused to let him come to her place after the club, David had called Amber, pretending to be interested in her reaching her apartment safely.

Amber thought he was calling from home, but he had actually

called her from a payphone, not too far from her place. He had followed her, making sure her destination really was her apartment. He asked her out to an early dinner, or rather he told her they would be going to dinner.

"Oh, really?" Che was skeptical as she listened to Amber tell her story. She still didn't believe David was divorcing his wife. Furthermore, she didn't accept that his wife was out of town like he kept telling Amber. She knew the subject of Mr. David's wife was a taboo one with Amber and didn't plan on bringing it up. Instead she just cautioned her friend.

"You just make sure you watch yourself with that one, okay?"

"I can take care of myself. So, tell me..." Amber still wanted to find out more about Che and Malik, and Che could sense it. She smiled to herself.

"I'm not telling!" She joked with her friend. She could feel her curiosity through the phone.

"Okay, be that way! I gotta go anyway. I have to get ready for my hot date."

Amber didn't want Che to know how badly she really wanted to know what happened with her and Malik. Actually, she felt as if she already knew and just wanted confirmation of the obvious. It could come out sooner or later. Che was the kiss-and-tell type.

"I'll yak wit ya later, girl."

Amber and Che hung up the phone, and Amber went about getting ready for her date with David. She was surprised Che didn't seem in the least bit annoyed that she was going out with

David. Originally, Amber and Che were supposed to go to the movies together. She probably wasn't upset because she was going to meet some man herself. Amber hadn't really given her the chance to bring it up. It was probably Malik! What an asshole he turned out to be. He seemed to just latch right on to Che immediately. Che gave him every reason in the world to chase her; she was practically laying the pussy on the table for him.

Amber showered, and as she finished, she glanced at her watch. She was surprised David hadn't arrived already. He was 15 minutes late. Maybe the stint of good behavior was over. She thought about him as she continued dressing. She was so deep in thought that when the phone rang, she didn't get to it until the third ring. She usually answered so fast sometimes the person on other end never heard it ring.

"Hello?"

"Hey, sweetness!" It was David. "Do you want the good news or bad first?"

"You're not coming." Amber tried not to sound disappointed.

"I didn't say that. Actually, I'm going to be late. Can I pick you up at seven instead? I have to work late." Amber glanced at her watch. Seven was still an hour away.

"Okay, fine. I'll be waiting." She hung up, thinking that at least he wasn't standing her up. Lots of folks wouldn't even have the decency to call.

Amber continued getting dressed and turned on the television. She sat down to wait for David. Time passed, and before long, seven o'clock had come and gone. At eight, Amber hadn't heard from David and began to wonder what the deal was. Instead of being upset she thought he was probably still working and would call her later. She sat in front of the television until well past midnight, sipping on flat, leftover wine. Finally, wine-induced tiredness took over. She undressed and went to bed. As she lay in bed, she thought about how long it had been since she had been stood up. Married people generally didn't get stood up.

By noon the next day, Amber still had not heard from David. He wasn't at the gym, either. Amber called Che and couldn't resist telling her about the incident, waiting for her to say "I told you so." Instead, to Amber's surprise, she reassured her.

"I'm sure there is some good explanation." Amber raised her eyebrows. Che surprised her sometimes.

"You're probably right."

Che was in a good mood as she listened to Amber. She tried to make her friend feel better, although she felt as if David's standing Amber up was just a manifestation of his true character. Amber made him feel too secure, and he was beginning to take advantage of her, just as Che thought he would. She knew that all men were the same, deep down. Maybe not even so deep. Too bad Amber couldn't see it. In spite of what she really thought, she was going to do her good Samaritan deed for the day and stroke Amber's hurt ego.

"He'll probably call you today." She tried to change the subject. "I talked to Malik today, he has some questions about your assignments. He said he was going to call your voice mail at school, but I gave him your number. He didn't want to call you at home. He is almost as proper as you!"

Amber knew she had his number on her roster, or did he give it to her? She couldn't remember. She usually transposed all of that information into her electronic organizer.

"I'll give him a call as soon as I find my electronic organizer. Did I leave it over at your place?" Amber realized she really had not seen the organizer since David moved her into her new place. She couldn't find her roster either.

"I can just give you his number. And no, I haven't seen that thing! I hope you didn't leave it anywhere. Someone will have all your business."

Amber walked her friend to the door and watched her as she went down the walk to her car. As she watched her go, she thought about Che's reassuring words concerning David and was not quite convinced. If there was such a good explanation, why hadn't he called yet? His fingers better be broken or something!

Amber began to pick up her apartment, which was a mess. As she was cleaning, the phone rang. He was finally calling! She ran over and grabbed the phone, and as she answered, she tried her best to sound relaxed and unconcerned.

"Hello?"

Amber was expecting it to be David, but instead it was Malik.

"Oh, hi Malik."

"Don't sound so glad to hear from me."

"I was expecting someone else."

"Sorry, I'm not him," Malik said cheerfully. Che still hadn't told Amber what happened, but by now, she knew that Malik had become one of Che's one night stands.

"What can I do for you?" she asked.

"I thought that maybe you would be interested in going to the museum with me?"

"Excuse me! I am your teacher and you hung out with my best friend! Aren't you guys kickin' it now? Shouldn't you ask Che that question?" He must think that she was stupid!

"What?", he asked, surprised.

"Don't you think you should be taking Che? I mean, didn't you two...?"

"No, we did not! I just took her home! She's not my girlfriend now or anything. Hold on a minute. I got a call."

Malik clicked over without waiting for her response.

Maybe they really hadn't spent the night together. That would explain Che's almost outright refusal to tell her the details, she always loved to tell Amber the down and dirty. Maybe there were no details.

Malik came back on the line.

"I'm sorry. That was another one of those weird calls. They never say anything."

"Yeah, okay. I'll go." Maybe a trip to the museum would take her mind off David. Besides if he did call her, it would probably be better if she weren't home. He would be the one waiting for a change.

"Great. I'll pick you up in an hour. Are you sure your boyfriend won't mind you going to Houston with me? I don't want to cause any trouble." There was a hint of mischief in Malik's voice.     "Wait, boy. You didn't say anything about Houston. What's wrong with Austin's museum?"

"Nothing. There are a few museums, right there together, in Houston, Africa-girl." He said, laughing. "What's the matter; afraid of a road trip, or afraid to be alone with me? I don't want you to get no whippin's or anything like that."

"Don't flatter yourself. I'll be here!" Amber hung up and began to get ready to go.

# 26

MALIK AND AMBER were silent during their trip to Houston. The silence should have been awkward but instead was comfortable for them both, like they were old friends and this unexpected roadtrip was something they did often. They had a good time, with Amber showing Malik around the museum. She had never been there but she knew a lot about art. When she spent her summer in New York, she spent a great deal of time at the Metropolitan Museum of Art.

During their visit, Amber stopped to check her messages several times and still there was no message from David. After awhile, she and Malik were really enjoying themselves, so she stopped worrying about David and stopped checking her machine. They stayed at the museum until closing time, and then headed back to the parking lot.

"You have any plans for dinner? We should eat here, Austin is so far away." Malik looked down at his shoes, as if they were guiding him back to the car.

Amber looked at her watch. What plans did she have? David didn't give two shits about her, that was obvious. She might as well.

"You're probably right. What did you have in mind?"

"Well, do you like sushi?"

Amber didn't answer him at first; she was really surprised. Sushi sounded pretty sophisticated for Malik. She had taken him for a real country bumpkin. Obviously, that was a mistake. Actually, Amber considered herself a woman of the world, just like LaShaun used to say, but she had not actually experienced sushi.

"Well, I think that I might. I like fish and stuff, but I've never really had any, except for salad bar California rolls." She smiled at Malik. And she thought he was a country bumpkin.

"Well, I know this place I think you'll like. Don't worry, I'll guide you in the right direction!"

"Hey, I thought you didn't know your way around the city!"

"Well, not exactly," Malik started the car. "I said I didn't know my way around the art museum. You assumed the rest."

Malik took Amber to a small, informal restaurant. It was

tucked back in the corner of a dead end street that was so narrow it looked more like an alley to Amber. All of the seats were arranged around a circular sushi bar, with the chefs in the middle. The rest of the place had a real down-home feel that was more Korean than Japanese, but neither of them knew it.

They sat at the bar and Amber felt totally out of place. She didn't know what to do. The chefs were preparing the sushi and placing it on little boats. The sushi bar had a moat in it, and the boats would float by. As they did, the sushi-eaters would grab things that interested them. Amber was amazed; everything seemed to be happening so fast, and none of the food looked familiar.

"Okay," she finally said to Malik. "What am I supposed to do?" She had no idea what she was supposed to grab first.

"Let me—, "Anticipating her hesitation, Malik began to grab the sushi boats as they floated past, explaining to Amber what each piece was as he did. Amber was amazed, and pretty soon the two of them were laughing together as Amber missed several grabs at the moving boats. She soon got the hang of it and quickly learned what she liked and what she didn't. They stayed at the bar quite awhile, grabbing their food as it floated by.

"So, What did you think?" Amber grew more comfortable with Malik during dinner, and they were now on the way home.

"I think I had more fun fishing for the food than eating it!" They laughed about the mess she had made attempting to catch her food.

"Now, that's my idea of fishing!"

Amber had really enjoyed herself. Malik was definitely much
cooler than she anticipated, he was certainly too sophisticated for
Che. Her dinner experience made her realize there was no way he
could possibly be interested in her friend, at least not seriously.
Still, that wasn't to say the two of them couldn't have had a one-
night stand. Even the most sophisticated men were known to
think with their dicks once in awhile. She doubted he was any
exception.

For most of the ride home, they discussed the art museum and
the differences between the museum in Houston and other
museums they had visited.

"I had no idea you were so knowledgeable about art. You
don't look the type."

"Oh? I appreciate beauty wherever I see it," Malik answered.

Amber was silent; they were almost home and it seemed as if
they just left the restaurant.

"Feel like coming over for a drink?"

All of Amber's alarms went off. She should have seen it
coming. Still, she did have a good time and did not want to insult
Malik.

"I don't think I should…," Malik cut her off.

"Hey, I promise, I won't bite, just a drink. Besides, I haven't
had any real guests since I moved in. You got something else to
do?"

Amber contemplated his offer. Why the fuck not? It would

be better than sitting home and waiting for David to show up. She accompanied Malik to his apartment, which was similar in layout to hers. It was furnished impeccably, which did not surprise Amber. He always looked together, so why should his apartment be any different?

He lit the fireplace, and they laughed and joked as wine flowed freely. After awhile, Malik stopped smiling. Amber could tell he was about to ask her something serious.

"So Africa, what do you see in Mr. David?" She was up to her third or fourth glass of wine and replied without hesitating.

"Whaddya mean?"

"What I mean is, he doesn't seem like your type. He doesn't seem to care about anyone but himself!"

"How would you know, you don't know him!" Amber was a little annoyed, how dare this guy who knew nothing about her make judgments about her friends!

"Calm, down. Maybe I don't know him, but I know his type. He's a little, well, Cro-magnum. Besides, I probably know him a little better than you think. I can tell your type too, I have a knack for that type of thing." Malik had piqued her interest.

"Oh, yeah? What type am I, exactly?"

Malik paused and then spoke softly.

"Well," he said, "You are the type who is very insecure inside, but you try to make everyone think you are very sure of yourself."

She tried to interrupt; maybe she didn't' really want to hear this after all.

"I'm not done. You also have this idea of the way you think you should be, the way things should be, and you try to make them that way, even if it is uncomfortable."

"Really!?" Amber didn't know if she should be insulted or not.

"Yeah, really." Malik paused again to take another sip of his wine. "And, *why* are you friends with Che?"

"Excuse me? Do you have anything good to say about any of my friends?!"

Amber couldn't believe Malik, he really hadn't known her that long. Now he was dissecting all of her relationships.

"Let me rephrase that, what I mean is, is she really your friend?"

He looked at Amber, waiting for her answer. She was flustered and didn't know what to say. She felt as if he looked right through her, into her soul, the way old people did back home. Amber felt naked, the way she often did when she talked to her grandmother, whom she never had been able to hide anything from, or like she did when her dad looked into her eyes.

"You have some nerve! I thought I was the one with the psychology degree! Can we talk about something else?"

"This ain't about psychology, Africa. You know as well as I do that it is about knowing. That's all."

He touched on some sensitive subjects, and Amber really didn't want to talk about it. Actually, she was annoyed because he hit every nail right on the head. She had yet to admit it, but she was very insecure. She did spend a lot of time trying to hide it from people. For once in her life, she did not feel in control as much as she wanted to be. As for David, he was getting on her nerves more and more lately, but it wasn't his fault, was it? He still excited her sexually, but lately he was seriously messing up.

Amber stayed at Malik's place, and they talked most of the night. Finally, the wine began to take over, and they fell asleep in front of the fire. When the fire went out, Malik got up and covered Amber with a blanket. She was so tired, she didn't even realize he was gone. When she finally awoke, it was daylight, and Malik was in the next room, cooking. At first, Amber was confused. She didn't remember where she was.

""Want some breakfast?" Malik smiled at Amber.

"Is it morning?" she asked, confused. "Why didn't you wake me so I could go home?" Amber looked around the room at the empty wine bottle, then down at herself. She had to make sure that she still had her clothes on.

"Don't worry, I was a gentleman."

Amber smoothed out her blouse and retrieved her shoes from underneath the sofa. This mind-reading stuff was getting annoying. She looked at Malik preparing breakfast. Where was she rushing off to? It's not like anyone was at her place waiting for her. She watched him work and the smells coming from the kitchen got her stomach going. She may as well stay for breakfast. He continued cooking as Amber watched, producing fluffy omelets, just the way Amber liked them. They had breakfast together and talked until noon.

While they ate, Amber watched Malik. He really was a gentleman. She could not remember the last time she met someone like him. She thought about the conversations they had last night and at the art museum. She really had a good time and enjoyed getting to know him. As she sat there and watched him, she realized there was no way he and Che could get together. They were too different. Amber thanked Malik for a wonderful afternoon, evening, and night. He walked her to the door, and to Amber's surprise, he even helped her with her jacket. It was cooler than it had been lately.

As she walked home, she felt refreshed and didn't give David one thought. For once, she met someone who didn't appear to want anything from her, and she liked it.

# 27

DAVID DECIDED TO CALL Amber a whole 24 hours later.
When he got her answering machine after three tries, he went by
her apartment. When he got there, her car was still in its place.

Since her car was in its parking space, the only explanation was
she just must have not been answering the phone. It was now his
turn to knock on Amber's door. He stood outside her apartment
for 45 minutes, and then began to get worried. What if she were
inside the apartment and something happened to her? He
couldn't let himself in like he was accustomed to; Amber took her
key back after their last disagreement.

Eventually, David went back to his place, called 911 and all the area hospitals. He even called Che, thinking that Amber might be at her place. Che told him she wasn't there and didn't know where she could be. Finally, not knowing what else to do, he drove over to Che's place. Maybe she was hiding Amber or something.

Che was sitting around, watching television when David unexpected knocked on her door.

"Is Amber here?"

David looked past Che into apartment. Che was a little surprised because every other time she saw David, he appeared calm and collected. Besides, hadn't he called earlier?

Was this Tyler all over again or what?

"I told you I didn't know where she was when you called. Didn't you believe me?"

David looked Che up and down, and then sighed.

"What if something is wrong? She never goes anywhere without letting someone know where she is going!"

Che knew that wasn't true, at least not anymore. David pushed past Che and walked into her apartment without being asked. Che followed him to the sofa and watched as he sat down and put his head in his hands. She was sure Amber was all right, but what could she be up to?

"Look, you know what they say, no news is good news. If something were wrong, one of us would have heard." She offered him a drink, hoping to calm his nerves.

David hung around and watched television with Che; soon his

emotions changed from concern to anger.

"How dare she stay away and not call or something!" He did not mention he stood Amber up for a date. Che began to feel genuinely sorry for him. As they sat there, they commiserated, and the alcohol began to comfort him. His closeness reminded Che how sexy he really was. "Why did Amber get all the good ones?" she thought.

About an hour passed and soon their conversation drifted from Amber.

"So just what was it you thought you were doing when you came to my office the other day?"

Che was surprised by his question. She hadn't mentioned the incident to Amber or anyone else, instead she pushed it to the back of her mind. At the time, her intent was to come between David and Amber, perhaps destroying their relationship. She was jealous, but she was not about to admit that to David.

"Whaddya mean? Maybe I was just testing you. I gotta look out for my girl!" She smiled at David. His mind was obviously no longer on finding Amber.

Che was a lot nicer than he thought. She didn't really breathe fire after all, just smoke! He moved closer to Che, and as he did, she moved backward.

"Um, What are you doing?" Che was caught off guard. If she didn't know better, she would think David was making a pass at her. David moved toward Che and kissed her. He was very tentative at first.

"Do you know what you are doing? Are you sure that this is what you what?" Che couldn't believe it! She was kissing her best friend's man.

"I don't do things I don't mean," he said. To Che, it was as if he were using his sexiest voice ever. She laughed before when Amber described his voice, comparing him to Teddy Pendergrass and all that, now she understood where Amber was coming from. David kissed Che again, this time forcefully.

David fondled Che's breasts, eventually putting his hand inside her blouse. He continued to kiss her as he undid her bra.

They continued to get busy on the sofa, and David got rougher and rougher. Che was pleased; not only would she have dirt on David, but he was being sexually rough, the way she liked it. Amber never mentioned that part to her, she didn't know Amber liked it that way, too. Before long, Che helped David to remove most of her clothing. He continued to kiss her, moving to her breasts.

"Let's go to the bedroom."

She noted he was not wasting any time, she wasn't even wet yet. She picked up her clothing as she guided David to the bedroom. When they got there, she sat on the bed. David, walked behind her, hesitating slightly. Che watched him, noting he still had all of his clothes on.

"Excuse me," she said. 'Don't you believe in equal opportunity?" She reached for him as he stood beside the bed and began to unbutton his shirt. He placed his wallet on her table, on top of the copy of *One Dead Preacher* that was laying there. When he was finally undressed, she looked him up and down, from head to toe, noting the slight left curve in his penis.

"Ummh". No wonder Amber was so head over heels! He probably rocked her world with that!

Che had no idea where Amber was, but at this point, she didn't care. What her friend missed out on by playing her hide and seek games, she was about to gain. David hesitated as she admired him. He fell back on the bed, leaving Che motionless.

"This isn't right." He said. "We should be ashamed. " David stood up and began to dress himself.

Che looked at him dressing, all of the effects of the alcohol he was drinking seemed to have left him. How could he leave like this?

"You are just making excuses. Mr. Macho isn't a real man after all." David swung around to face Che.

"You, bitch! You don't even know what you're talking about! You ain't a real woman either, or should I say friend?"

"I know that you are standing there with a limp dick after getting me all fired up! If you had a problem getting it up, you should have said so!" Che's words hit home. David's face became dark with anger.

"Please, what makes you think I would want your nasty ass, anyway? It was just going to be a revenge fuck, because I was mad at your friend. I took one look at you and couldn't stand the thought. Your body was an instant turnoff!"

Che picked up the rest of his clothes and began to throw them at David.

"Just get the hell out of here!" She screamed as David ran toward the door. "Get out! Wait until I tell your precious Amber about this, you asshole, just wait!"

David never answered Che, he finally reached the door. She fumed as he opened it, running out into the parking lot. Some motherfuckin' nerve. Che looked over at the sofa, where they had been sitting and noticed that David had left his wallet. She didn't think twice as she sat down and dumped the contents onto the coffee table.

If he was supposed to be so well to do, where were the credit cards? Che was no longer angry as she went through the contents of David's wallet. She noticed there were no credit cards in his wallet, and no money. In fact, the only thing in the wallet that Che felt to be of any significance was a Blockbuster video membership card.

She was about to put the wallet back together when she noticed a red ID card. Che flipped it over, she recognized it as military ID card, an expired one. Funny, she thought. Amber hadn't mentioned that David was in the military. After her experience with Tyler and all the complaining she did about moving around the country, Che was surprised Amber would even date anyone even remotely associated with the military.

Che examined the ID card. The next thing she saw caused her mouth to drop open. She read the card out loud. "Eyes, green. Hair brown. Race. CAUCASIAN!"

Caucasian! Amber was seriously holding out. No, she obviously did not know this juicy tidbit. David was white. He sure had everyone fooled. Ole girl would definitely be shocked, maybe this would get rid of David for good.

Che put the wallet back together, leaving out the ID card. She might need this for proof later. As she folded the wallet over, Che thought about how often Amber had mentioned her father and her family's thoughts about interracial dating. As light-skinned as Amber was, she definitely had hang-ups about skin color and race. Not that it mattered to Che, she had her share of white men. That type of thing just didn't matter when the lights were out. Che laughed to herself. Amber's knight in shining armor wore white, both inside and out! Amber would absolutely die. She could still taste him.

# 28

AMBER GOT BACK to her apartment and immediately took a shower. She felt grungy because she slept in her clothes all night. She couldn't believe it, not only did she sleep on the floor all night, she had done so at some guy's apartment with whom she was not romantically involved with, at least not yet. As usual, she planned to call Che and tell her about her weekend, by now she would know she had been up to something. Amber knew Che would never believe nothing happened between her and Malik. Why should she? Amber hadn't believed Che hadn't slept with him either. She knew for sure now the two of them probably hadn't been together. Not that she was about to admit it to Che.

Che wouldn't believe her because Che's mind was always in the gutter. Amber didn't believe Che because her body was often there, too.

After she was dressed, Amber went to call Che. She carefully thought about what she was going to say; she wanted to make sure she would keep Che in as much suspense as possible. She also knew it would be useless to call Che too early — she would be where she always was on Sunday mornings, in church. Usually Amber went too, if she felt like it. It depended on which choir was singing. If the gospel choir was singing, then Amber would surely be there; it always left the church rockin'. Otherwise, she could take it or leave it. Music was one of the reasons she joined the church when she did. In fact, she joined on a Sunday when the gospel choir was singing. When the other choir sang, they were so boring, it often put Amber to sleep. The choir members didn't clap or sway or anything during any of their selections. Most of the members of that choir were older, and many were so farsighted they couldn't read the music. They just weren't together, and this was a big turnoff for Amber. Music was important to her; it was part of the church experience.

Growing up, Amber's father encouraged her to listen to and appreciate a variety of music. Her father's appreciation for music helped Amber to develop a sincere appreciation it, as long as the music was good. And the regular church choir had a tendency to be very far from good, even downright bad.

Although Amber's dad taught her to appreciate music, he

never encouraged her to pursue anything in the arts, at least not as a profession. For fun, he taught her to play the keyboard. In high school, he let her take guitar lessons to fulfill a music requirement, but that is where it stopped. Once, someone told her she had a pleasant voice, and Amber wanted to take singing lessons. She asked her father if she could, and he had hit the roof! He started to rant and rave about not wanting any "buck dancing" and "sangin'" niggers in his house. He told her to study her science and her math instead, and of course she did. Her father assured her that if she did that, she would always have something to fall back on. But she at least she could go on loving music.

Most of the time, the members of the church congregation would sit and listen politely to the choir, clapping when the choir finally finished. Amber would think they were clapping for joy, but there was only so much she could take. She figured out the number of "Amen's" and "sang-it Sisters" was directly proportional to how bad the soloist was that day. As it got worse, the amount of vocal praise from the congregation went up. Finally, she tried to attend church only on days when she knew that the music would be good. She found she could concentrate on the message as opposed to how bad the choir was.

Even though she had officially joined the church, Amber didn't believe it was necessary to be there every Sunday, unlike Che. That would be too Catholic.

Amber thought about Che and chuckled to herself. Her

friend was most definitely the "sinning-est sinner". She would always raise hell on Saturday night, and the rest of the week for that matter, and was the first one in church on Sunday. Sometimes she would stay all day, making sure that everyone saw her praising the Lord. She was one case where the stereotype about the preacher's daughter was true.

As she walked past her answering machine, Amber noticed her message light was flashing. She stopped and played back her messages and all but one of them were from David. He had left four messages, and the last two sounded kinda urgent. At first he sounded apologetic for not showing up. By the last message, his tone changed. He was mad. Obviously, he couldn't believe she was not home. He surely didn't think she would sit around and wait for him all weekend! Amber knew that if Malik had not invited her out, she really might have stayed around and waited, right by the phone.

Amber dialed Che's number. The last message was from her friend, apparently David called her, so by now she would know definitely Amber stayed out all night.

"Girl, where have you been?" Amber could sense Che's excitement.

"Out."

"All weekend?" Che sounded annoyed, but Amber wasn't sure.

"Yes, all weekend. I had a date with David, and he didn't show. So I decided to give him some of his own medicine!"

"Oooh, girl! You know you're wrong! So what did you do?"

Amber thought about how much she was actually going to tell Che. Sometimes it was best to leave some things to the imagination.

"Well," she said. "I went to Houston." Amber paused a minute. "With Malik." She waited for a response but instead she heard Che pause and draw in her breath.

"Did you hear me? I went to Houston with Malik, to the art museum. Then we had sushi…"

"Sushi? As in raw fish?" Che asked. "You do know sushi is supposed to be a natural aphrodisiac?"

"Yeah, I know, but I'm not done. Then he got me drunk and I spent the night at his house." Amber ran this part all together.

"You didn't!"

Amber smiled. Che was the one who was shocked for a change.

"Yes, I did, but nothing happened. Actually, I fell asleep and he just left me there." Amber waited for Che's disbelief. She knew it was coming.

"Am I supposed to believe that you slept at over his house and he didn't touch you?"

Amber sighed. She knew Che wouldn't believe her. Maybe she was mad; she tried to put her claws in Malik first. Or maybe she was jealous, she still sometimes got a little bent out of shape when she hung out with other people.

"We didn't DO anything. He really is a gentleman!"

Che didn't really care where Amber was all weekend. Actually, she was toying with Amber. She had juicier information, but she wanted to wait. Amber didn't deserve to know she had discovered that David was really white, or had at least said he was on his ID card. Whatever the case, it would have the same effect. Either he was passing for Black (that's a switch!), or he was passing for White. Either would be an unforgivable sin in Amber's eyes. No, she would hold that information for later.

"Well, you know your crazy boyfriend was looking all over town for you. He called the police, and guess what?"

Now it was Amber's turn to be silent as Che toyed with her some more.

"What?" She waited. Amber could sense that Che was holding back purposely.

"He even came by my house, girl. He was mad! And he was worried. Why did you have to do him that way?"

Amber laughed to herself. Still, she knew something was up. Her eyes narrowed.

"He deserved it, you know he did. So what happened?" Again she waited. This was too normal. There had to be a twist somewhere.

Che knew Amber sensed that there was more to the story, but she was not ready to burst her friends bubble yet. She wanted her to wait. Besides, now David wasn't good enough for her anymore, it looked like she was moving in on Malik, too.

"What do you mean what happened? I calmed him down and sent him on his way. You know, that boy is really crazy about you."

Amber was satisfied. What had she been thinking?

"Is he really?"

"Yeah. Besides, you're right. He did deserve it. What's good for the goose is good for the gander, isn't that what they say?" They both laughed again, this time almost shrieking. Che smirked to herself. It sure was.

The two friends chatted together, each thinking she had gotten the best of the other, but neither knew the whole story, or was willing to admit to anything.

# 29

MALIK WAS TRULY A GENTLEMAN; Amber really did spend
the night in his house, and he hadn't attempted anything. Maybe
she was losing it. Could it be Malik didn't find her attractive?
Not that she really wanted anything to happen; Amber kind of
liked the prospect of a friendship with Malik, and sometimes sex
with friends ruined everything. Besides, she really was crazy about
David, even though she was still angry at him for standing her up
the way he had.

Who says all men are dogs? She and Malik seemed to hit it
off, even if he made her feel as if he were looking through her. He
was able to see through all of the walls she normally put up

between herself and others. The only other person seemed to be able to look through her was her grandmother, but that was expected; she was old and had seen just about everything.

This was a little uncomfortable, she was not used to disclosing her private thoughts to people, and Malik put her on the spot several times, almost forcing her to be truthful, even if it were just to herself.

As she was taking her shower, she also thought about David. If he was so worried about her while she was gone this past weekend, why wasn't he waiting at her doorstep when she got home? Instead he went crying to Che.

Stepping out of the shower, Amber heard the doorbell ring. She made her way to the door and checked the peephole. She had finally talked with David, and when she did, he invited himself over. He sounded really pissed off on the phone. He apparently thought he had a right to be angry with her.

David walked into the living room without saying hello. He strutted around the room. To Amber it looked like he seemed to be checking for evidence of someone else having been there.

"Hey. And how are we today?"

"Excuse me, David?"

"I asked how you were. I was a little concerned, since it seems you were having difficulty answering your phone. And door. And finding a phone."

"I wasn't aware I had to check in." Amber was sure now he was jealous without even knowing where she had been.

"So, where were you?"

"Didn't I say I wasn't aware I had to let you know where I was? None of your business."

"Oh, I see. It's like that, huh? Is that the thanks I get for all I have done for you?"

Amber recognized what David was trying to do. He wanted to turn all of the focus for the blame on her so, overshadowing whatever he had done. Amber was quite familiar with the tactic because Tyler had done it to her for 10 years.

"You've got some nerve, if you were really worried about my welfare, you would have called me!"

She was furious with David and wanted him to know it. She had better things to do than sit around and wait for him. Amber couldn't hold back her tears. She began to cry; screaming at David as she did.

"So where were you? What was her name? I'm sure you have some real good excuse!"

David looked at Amber, and as always, he immediately softened at the sight of her tears. He moved toward her and put his arms around her. Amber tried to pull away but David wouldn't let her.

"I'm sorry, I meant to call you and tell you what was going on. But I was so excited that the time got away from me." His voice was soft and low. He used his forefinger to dry her tears as they ran down her face.

Amber sniffled. Why couldn't she just be angry with David

like anyone else would? Why did she always have to cry?

Amber had planned what she was going to say so well, but she knew she wouldn't be able to say any of it. She hadn't put any tears into her script, and here they were anyway.

Amber stood there in David's arms and watched his reaction to her tears. For a minute she actually felt bad about crying in front of him. It was as if tears actually gave her the upper hand in the argument.

She thought about her father. Her tears always affected him the same way they affected David when she was a child. Whenever she got in trouble, she would start to sniffle and then cry. Her father would always give her a lecture. At the end of his long tirade, he would proclaim whatever the punishment was going to be. Amber figured out if she cried before he got to the end of his speech, she would never be punished or whipped. Her dad would get the same look on his face David did, and eventually his voice would soften. Before long, Amber's father was doing the apologizing, just like David was now. To this day, she held the distinction of being the only kid on her block who had never gotten a whipping from her parents.

She used to brag about her un-beat status, and often would instruct the other kids on what to do so they could avoid beatings too. Funny, now you couldn't even whip your kids, they would say it was child abuse, and some kids were even bringing their parents up on charges or trying to divorce them.

Standing there with David, Amber also thought about her

brother. He never caught on quite as quickly as Amber had to the science of avoiding beatings. As a result, he was always on punishment. He often got whipped worse than he normally would have; he went in the entire opposite direction than Amber. He had just refused to cry. He would stand his ground, without blinking an eye. This often made their father get angrier, and he would whip harder, trying to make the boy react. Amber's brother would stand his ground until he absolutely, positively couldn't take it anymore. At that point, he wouldn't yell or anything. He would just cry one tear. What did that prove? His butt would be whipped good by then. Boys sure were dumb.

Amber had tried this trick with her father until she was well past the whipping age. She thought it would work with her grandmother too. She soon found out that it didn't. Grandma would make Amber go into the yard and pick her own switch. She didn't even lecture the way Amber's father did. When Amber began to cry, she just looked at her and waited for her to be done, and then she would whip her. Amber would sometimes try to be slick and break up the switch at intervals so it would wrap around her instead of hit her real hard. Her grandmother would make her get another one. Or worse yet, she would use the flyswatter, hitting Amber right across her legs. Amber was one of the few people in creation actually glad that someone had the foresight to create the electric bug zapper.

After a couple of months of Grandma's whippings, Amber forgot about how effective tears could be on some people. But as

David kept trying to dry her tears while he explained where he had been, Amber remembered. She smiled inside, but outside she cried harder, throwing in the required sniffle. As she turned on the waterworks, Amber watched David become more and more uncomfortable. She realized she was enjoying manipulating him.

"I'm sorry I didn't call," David said again. "But something really special happened. I found my real father."

Amber snapped back to the present. She remembered David telling her he was adopted and didn't know who his real parents were.

"What!? How did that happen?" Amber forgot both her anger and her tears.

"Yeah, he lives in Oklahoma."

Amber looked into David's eyes and he looked away. Still, she could see his excitement.

"How did you find him?"

"Actually, he found me. I got this call, before we were supposed to meet. I was so excited I forgot about our appointment. I hope you'll forgive me. I know I've been messing up lately. "

Amber looked at David. His eyebrows were raised and he was pouting a little. He sounded so sincere that she had to give in.

"How do you know he was real your father. What did he say?" Amber was skeptical. This sounded like another one of David's too-good-to-be-true stories.

"He says that he had an affair with my mother, who he claims was white. And she was married. That makes sense. How many white men you know would raise their white wife's black baby? That's why they had to give me up. That's where I was, I mean, I went to see him. But I sure missed you." David began to kiss Amber's face.

She squirmed in his arms. Amber couldn't believe it. Although the story was a little incredible, she wanted to believe him. And David felt so damn good hugging her like that. She began to kiss him back.

"If it makes you happy, fine. I mean, I'm glad if it makes you happy," she said as they hugged.

David spent several hours telling Amber about his encounter with his father. Amber shared in his excitement; he had such a sexy smile that Amber couldn't help but enjoy seeing him happy. During their whole conversation, David avoided looking directly at Amber. Every time she looked in his eyes, he would look away. Amber noticed, but didn't say anything to him. She sensed he wasn't telling her everything, but didn't want to push the issue, at least not then.

Finally, their conversation turned away from the weekend's events and they began to make love, right there on the couch. Amber never thought about David having stood her up. The only thing she was able to think about was what was going on at that very moment; he knew how to touch Amber in all the right spots.

David always liked to start by going down on Amber; he knew it was a prerequisite to putting Amber in just the right mood. If he did it right, they would make love for hours.

Halfway through their foreplay, Amber realized she was not thinking about David, instead her thoughts were on Malik.

"If I am so sexy to David, why not to Malik, too?" She thought. "Maybe Malik is gay."

Amber continued contemplating the events of the prior weekend. She was so pensive eventually David began to notice she wasn't responding to him as usual.

"What's wrong?" He said. "Are you still mad? I said I was sorry." David's voice pulled Amber back to the matter at hand.

"No, I'm not mad, David. I was just really disappointed. I missed you." She kissed him long and hard, and soon he seemed to have forgotten she had been distant. Once again, Amber began to enjoy David's skill at lovemaking. She relaxed and enjoyed herself, pushing her encounter with Malik to the back of her head.

# 30

OVER THE NEXT COUPLE OF WEEKS, Amber tried to concentrate her energies more on herself and her teaching than on David. She wanted to finish the semester feeling that she had done a good job. They still went out on the weekends, but during the week Amber spent more time on her professional life. He often dropped by her place unannounced whether or not she was there.

Although Amber did not see David as much, she was still very much attracted to him. She just didn't have time. Mostly they saw each other in the gym.

For awhile, they stopped working out together, but Amber

soon felt herself getting soft. She could always see it in her legs first. She needed David's motivation. She wanted to be in the best physical shape possible for summer.

So now, after months of working out religiously, Amber's body was showing the results. She purposely picked her worst outfits to highlight her best features. As she dressed for the gym she studied her reflection in the mirror.

"Eat your heart out, Tyler." She preened and talked at her reflection. If he could see her now he sure would miss her. He definitely would be sorry the next time they met. It seems like every woman who gets a divorce looks better afterwards, and the men don't.

Amber also felt good about herself, and David made her feel beautiful. It had been that way when they first met, and it was still that way. He used to tell her the things Tyler should have been telling her all along. But unlike her soon-to-be-ex-husband, he kept telling her those things. Amber knew sometimes he was definitely full of shit when he laid those lines on her, but she still loved the attention.

Valentine's Day was next week, and she knew David would have something very romantic up his sleeve. Amber smiled as she thought about it, trying to imagine what his surprise would be. He could be very creative.

Amber and Malik were starting to become very good friends. There was no romantic involvement between them and that suited Amber just fine. He was a friend, sort of like Che, but without the animosity between them. They made a habit of having lunch together after class.

Malik often told Amber exactly what he thought about things, especially about her, and Amber liked that. She always knew exactly where she stood with him. And although he shared a lot of his personal feelings with her, Amber did not share quite as much with him.

She probably told him more about her thoughts than anyone else, but she still had not learned to be totally open with anyone. This arrangement suited them both; Malik just accepted her the way she was.

He made no secret he did not like David but that was all he told Amber. Once, while they were at lunch, Malik began to talk about David, seemingly out of the blue.

"He's a dirtbag, you know." He stated this matter-of-factly, as if Amber should know who he was talking about. The funny thing was she did know. It was as if they were often on the same wavelength lately.

"No, I didn't know," she replied. "What makes you an expert?"

"Let's just say that we've met before."

"Yeah, at the club. I introduced you, remember?" Sometimes Malik could be so cryptic. Why couldn't he just get to the point?

"Actually, that wasn't the first time."

That was the end of the conversation. Amber tried and tried, but all she could get out of Malik was that he and David had met before. He kept saying, "Believe me, just be careful." Then he changed the subject, just as suddenly as he had before.

During their lunches, Amber learned not to question Malik; eventually he would let her know what he was thinking. Amber wondered about the comments he made about David but couldn't quite get any more information out of him, so she just let it slide. She thought that maybe he made those comments because he was jealous; although they were just platonic friends, it was obvious he was attracted to her.

Amber found Malik attractive too, but it was very different from the attraction she felt for David. She just found Malik sexy. On the other hand, Amber admitted to herself that she was in love with David. In fact, he was probably the first person she really loved. When Amber was married to Tyler, she had not been in love with him. No doubt she loved him, but it was more like the love you have for an old pair of comfortable jeans you can't bring yourself to get rid of. It wasn't crazy-I'll-do-anything-for-you love, which is more what was between her and David.

Amber came to this realization during one of her conversations with Malik, and it made her very uncomfortable. She was not sure she liked the idea, or the way this new kind of love felt. She felt as if she were totally out of control, as if someone else had power over her and her actions. Hopefully, that someone else had good intentions. Although Amber's time was limited these days, she and David made the most of the time they did spend together. He began to come to her place regularly, often letting himself in. She had given him the key back about a week after he had reunited with his father. She felt he re-earned it. At first he would come in the evenings and then spend all night with Amber. They would watch television together or take long walks. David always had some kind of romantic plan.

David's car was still being fixed, so in the mornings, Amber drove him to work. This made her apprehensive, because David worked near where they used to live. However, she dropped him off not at the job but in the old neighborhood.

"They have an employee shuttle that picks up from here." David answered when she asked. She never bothered to wonder why he was always the only one waiting when she dropped him off.

Eventually his schedule changed and instead of him staying the night with her, he stayed all day. David would arrive in the morning, Amber would drop him off near his bus stop. In the evening, he said he was working nights to get a head start on the time difference between Austin and New York. Again, Amber never questioned him.

Amber finally got annoyed with the bus stop routine. The bus stop was on the other side of town.

"When are you getting your car back?" she snapped.

"Why? Don't you want to see me?"

"It's not that I don't want to see you, but every time I pick you up in the old neighborhood, I keep thinking I might run into some old neighbors."

"And...?" he asked.

"And Austin isn't that big. I don't want them starting rumors, that's all. It might be better if you drove yourself." She answered.

Amber knew it wouldn't be long before he would start asking to drive her car again. She wanted to head that off before it became an issue.

"You need to let me just drive your car..."

"Let's not even go there. We tried that before and you abused the privilege. When is your car coming back anyway?" Amber was angry.

David paused.

"Well," he said. "Let's just say it's not. It's gone."

Amber looked at David, confused. "Gone? What do you mean?"

"I mean, it's gone. As in repossessed. I forgot to pay the note, so they picked it up from the car repair place."

Amber couldn't believe what she was hearing. How does a working adult get his car repossessed? As long as she could remember, everyone in her family did whatever was necessary to pay their bills. She thought about her father, who always took bill paying and money very seriously. Every Friday, Amber would sit down at the dining room table, across from him as he balanced his checkbook and made sure the bills were paid properly, and on time. And her father didn't make half as much money as David claimed he did.

Money was very important to her. If she couldn't afford

something; she just went without rather than make a bill she couldn't pay.

"You must have forgotten quite a few payments!" She said.

"I was just busy, that's all. Trust me, I'll have a car tomorrow."

"Hmm! Whatever."

David not having a car was his problem, but she was not going to let him drive hers anymore.

Neither one of them mentioned the car again. The next day, true to his word, David drove up in a new car. It was a used Porsche that looked about three or four years old. It was a rusty tan color and was in excellent condition.

"Where did this come from?" Amber asked. She looked at the car in amazement.

"Want to ride?" David revved the engine as he spoke. Without answering, Amber hopped into the car. He handed her roses as she got in, but she couldn't focus on them.

"So, are you going to tell me where this came from?" She asked.

"Well, I had already called my folks when you asked me about my car. I had to have some way to get around to see my baby, right?" David leaned over and kissed Amber.

"So, you mean, you called your folks and asked them for money, and they sent you enough to get this?"

Amber was astonished. She could never imagine asking her father for money for something like a car. She couldn't imagine asking her father for money for much of anything.

When they got back to her house, David tickled Amber in some of her favorite spots with the rose petals. As it got dark, Amber asked David to stay the night.

"Can't," he said. "You know I have to work. I have a lot of catching up to do." He picked up his things, got in his new car and left.

Later that night, Amber was wide-awake, and wanted to talk to David. She picked up the phone, expecting to reach him at the office. She dialed his direct line, but it kept jumping to the night receptionist. She kept telling Amber that David was not available.

She drifted off to sleep, thinking the phone would wake her when David tried to return her call. Instead of being awakened by the phone, Amber woke up to the sunlight shining through her window, and the sounds of birds singing.

# 31

AMBER WAS ANGRY because David had not returned her call last night. She walked into her bathroom and flicked the light switch near her vanity mirror. Nothing happened. She flicked it again. Nothing. She walked back into her bedroom, and flicked a lamp switch. No light at all. In fact, there was no electricity anywhere in her apartment. She called the office, then the electric company. Apparently her bill had not been paid.

Amber had left the money to pay the bill with David, he offered to take care of it for her. At first she reasoned he must have forgot and misplaced it. Then the romance of trying to do everything by candlelight wore off. The shadows cast by the flickering candles that should have been saved for a sexy moment became menacing. Then Amber became furious. She knew the whites of her eyes were red if looked at them.

The next day, she got her lights turned back on after leaving a new deposit. A deposit she could barely afford. What else hadn't David taken care of? He must know what he did because Amber had not heard a peep out of him. It was nearing the end of the term, and not only did she have to study for her own exams, she needed to create some for the class she was teaching, too.

The electricity incident was hard enough to keep from Che; she kept trying to invite herself over to hang out. Amber used midterms as an excuse. She didn't feel much like company or hanging out. She even turned down the chance to go to a new Jazz club with Malik. That might have supplied some no-pressure fun but her heart just wasn't in it.

The ringing doorbell forced her to put the dish she was washing down. Amber waited as long as possible before answering the door, realizing that whomever was there was intent on seeing her. It was probably Che; she had kept her friend away as long as possible.

"Girl, I told you that I had stuff to..." She was stopped in mid-sentence.

"I ain't a girl, and what do you have to do that is more important than seeing me?"

Amber couldn't believe her eyes and ears. David was at the door, without calling first, acting like nothing was wrong. He wore the same old smile.

"I don't recall saying you could come over." She attempted to close the door, but David put his foot in the way.

"I didn't know I had to ask now. Let me come in, let me explain…"

He maneuvered his way into the apartment. Amber sighed. It was no use. She might as well hear what he had to say. She turned and walked away from he door, back towards the kitchen. David followed her without talking.

"Well…?"

"Damn, you hard, girl! The receptionist didn't know I was there. I let myself in the back way."

"David, I am not thinking about that. Tell me about my electric bill."

"Electric bill, uhm…"

"You heard me. Tell me why I sat in the dark for damn near two days!" Amber could feel her anger returning along with a headache.

"Oh, baby. I am sorry. I must have misplaced that bill and forgot all about it!"

Amber opened her mouth to speak, but the ringing doorbell cut her off.

"Who the hell is that?" She walked to the door and flung it open. "What do you want?! " She looked up and was surprised by an uniformed policeman standing there, poised to knock on the door as if he didn't expect the bell to have worked.

Amber's anger vanished. Somebody must be dead, and the police officer was coming to tell her.

"Yes??" she asked. She was unable to keep her voice from shaking.

"Ma'am. Excuse me. I am from the Travis County Sheriff's Department. I am looking for David Koppler. Is he here?"

Amber did not have time to answer. David was standing behind her, laughing a strained, very formal laugh.

"What's this about officer?" The officer stepped inside the door.

"David?" Asked the cop.

"Yes?" David started to back further into the apartment as he answered.

Another cop was suddenly behind him. Without answering, the first officer reached down and grabbed his handcuffs from his waist, moving Amber aside and handcuffing David in one movement.

"Son, you are under arrest for embezzlement and credit card fraud." He began to read David his rights. "You have the right to remain silent."

Amber couldn't believe what was happening in her entryway.

"You have the right to any attorney." Her mouth was open, and movement from the other policeman helped her find her voice.

"What is this about?" She asked after a moment. Her voice was shaking.

"Anything you say can and will be used against you in a court of law."

The other police officer stepped inside, moving Amber away from David.

"What's your name Miss?"

"Wait, I didn't do anything!"

She could feel herself beginning to sweat. Either that or she had lost control of her faculties and was pissing in her pants.

"Are you Amber LaReaux?"

Why was he asking her questions if he already knew the answers? He had papers in his hands. Although he was talking to her, all Amber heard was a Charlie Brown sort of voice with a Texas twang.

"Wah wah wah wah wah."

The papers were Amber's old phone bills. Apparently David had them for some reason. The cop was giving Amber some water. It cleared her head enough for her to understand David was a criminal. They were escorting David out and he was attempting to talk to her.

"Amber. Please." For the first time, Amber could see fear on David's face.

Please what? What did he want from her?

"Please, call my wife. Tell her. Let her know. Go see her. Please."

Amber's head whipped around on her shoulders. She couldn't believe what he was asking her. David wanted her to let his wife know what happened! He must be crazy. She stood there silently, as the police half escorted, half-pushed David out of her apartment. As far as she was concerned, she was pushing him out of her life. He kept talking to her, but she couldn't hear any of his words. The pounding in her head was deafening. Everything moved in slow motion. Then they were gone. Just like that.

Amber had no tears. A couple of weeks ago, she might have cried, but not now. She just sat on her sofa, staring. She knew the cop said he would be in touch, but for what? She wasn't sure. She sat there until night, and then she sat some more, without turning on any lights. Amber sat, motionless, until she sat herself to sleep.

# 32

THIS TIME I AM WATCHING *the person on the podium; I am no longer at the center. I know that the snake has already kissed me, and I can see with my eyes fine but I am still confused; more confused that ever. The storm is swirling around us, but it is only around me and the person on the podium that I can now tell is Malik. I am soaring above him with that strange out of body feeling. From here I can see my father, my family, outside the storm. They are all safe, but I can sense that I am not. They appear to be calling me.*

*"This is the worst storm yet."*

*It is Malik's turn to be kissed by the snake, but I do not understand this, he can already see. The people are dancing still, but they are also* outside the storm. The snake is no longer inside the basket; he is sitting on Malik's outstretched and open palm.

I can see that Malik's other hand is on top of the basket the snake was in, he appears to be holding the top on and the basket is shaking. Something inside is calling to me. "Marie!" I can even hear the voice calling me above the crescendo of the drums.

Malik is saying that I write the dance and I don't understand what he means; this makes no sense because this time I do not know the steps although he appears to. He moves his arm towards his face and the snake moves towards him too, grinning. I feel myself gasp as I realize that Malik is now as blind as I was and the music has stopped and the dancers have all passed out from exhaustion. Even the storm has stopped. Malik cannot see and I start to cry.

"Don't worry." He says. "Eyes don't really help you see at all." Why is he being cryptic again? I was feeling sorry for him when he should be feeling sorry for me. I want to help him but I know that he has to help himself.

"Kiss the snake again," I tell him. "The storm is over." He laughs at me and the snake laughs too. The basket is still yelling my name and I realize that the dancers must have created the storm.

"That will not help," he says. "It's not over, Africa; it is the eye of the storm."

# 33

LIKE A ZOMBIE, Amber was dazed through finals. It was a good thing she had already studied. She would not have been able to fit another thing inside her brain with all of the thinking she was doing about David. She listened to people leaving messages on her machine but did not want to talk to anyone.

"This is Che girl, call me." Beep.

"This is. Seton Hospital, please return the call." Beep.

"Amber! Where are you? I have stuff to tell you." Beep.

After her last exam, she couldn't take it anymore. She really wanted to talk to David's wife, not to help David, but instead to try and make sense of what was happening. She drove to his house, thinking about what she would say.

"Hi, I have been sleeping with your husband, but I thought you two had split up." She almost wanted to laugh at herself. How could she not have known? Everyone else probably did. She was probably the only one who believed David and his wife had really split up. Amber rang the doorbell. This time it opened promptly. David's wife was shorter than Amber remembered. She couldn't recall talking to her at all when she was a neighbor. Not ever. She was pretty and petite. Amber could not resist a glance at her hands; she immediately noticed her perfect French manicure on her perfect fiberglass overlays. Her hair was the same light brown color as Amber's, too.

"Um, hi." What was her name?

"I'm Jasmine. Come in. I knew I would be seeing you soon." Amber wondered what she meant by that. Had she known all along? She walked through the door. Nothing had changed inside the entryway and living room.

"Your name is Amber, right? I think you should sit down. You will need to, I think."

"Look, I don't want to bother you, I am just really confused. I should apolo…" Jasmine cut her off.

"Don't. Just save it. He was slick, you couldn't have known everything."

"What do you mean?' Amber was beginning to realize there was a lot she didn't see. She couldn't understand why Jasmine wasn't angrier with her. She knew she had a lot of nerve; coming up in her house like this, being the other woman and all.

"Did you know he had a problem?"

"Problem? Uh, no clue." She stuttered a little. Maybe she should have sat closer to the door.

"Yeah, he was sick. That's why he got kicked out of the military."

Jasmine was matter-of-fact, as if she told the story many times before. "After Desert Storm, he just flipped out, started acting crazy, doing stupid stuff."

Amber went over all of the things David had told her about his life and could not remember him even mentioning the military.

"They said it was post traumatic stress or something. He just became very irresponsible, spending money…"

"But he was doing good right? He was a stock broker, right?" Amber wanted something she knew to really be the truth. Jasmine paused, placing one slender hand on her hip.

"Stockbroker? That's a laugh! In Austin? He was a clerk at an investment firm…"

Her smile disappeared as quickly as it came. "He stole money from them, you know. Did some things in the computer. He was always real good at that. He transferred it into other people's accounts at night when he thought no one was around. David is crazy, but smart".

Amber was silent. Jasmine paused as if she were waiting for a response. She appeared to be studying Amber.

"Anyway, I started to try and dig up some more information

about his past, like, was this the first time he did stuff like this or what? It was too much, after he just didn't seem to care when I lost the baby, and he stole my credit cards and went skiing…"

Amber felt herself go paler than she already was. David had taken her skiing using stolen money! And did she say baby?

"You were pregnant?" She couldn't believe it! She remembered the card and his answer when she questioned him. He referred to his wife's miscarriage as 'some female thing'.

"Yes, yes, I was. Can I finish?" Jasmine was obviously getting annoyed. "Anyway, I tried to contact his parents…"

"Um, I don't understand. Couldn't you just call them?"

"Call them? They haven't spoken to us since we got married. Or at least not to me. They couldn't stand the thought of a Black daughter-in-law, much less any "half-Black" grandbabies."

Jasmine made quote signs as she moved her hands back and forth in the air like she was talking about the latest specials in the grocery store. Amber coughed, causing Jasmine to come closer.

"Oh, he didn't tell you that he was Black did he?" She didn't miss a beat, as if Amber's answer didn't matter. "He's done that before, you know."

Amber really didn't want to hear anymore, but was almost captive in the woman's house. "Oh?"

"Oh, yeah! Did he disappear for days at a time and break promises too?"

"Yeah."

"That's so classic. Didn't you ever wonder why he was so

secretive or why he didn't seem to remember things? Have you ever heard of multiple personality disorder?"

Amber felt so stupid. How could she not spot it? It was very rare in men. She thought back to David's unexplained disappearances and his weird behavior. He probably thought up some of those incredible stories he told to fill in the blanks where he couldn't remember things about his childhood.

"Now they call it Disassociative Personality…"

"Whatever." Jasmine gave Amber a look that told her that interrupting again might not be the best thing for her to do.

"Apparently he had that too. It started when he was younger. It doesn't go away. He was in therapy for years, and I didn't even know. He had an uncle who did terrible things to him when he was little…"

It was like the story was out of a textbook or something. She sat with Jasmine for an hour but Amber only heard snippets. She had been such an idiot; now she knew what people meant when they said love was blind. The whole thing was obvious to her now. Which one of David's personalities was so good in bed? Or had acted like she mattered to him? No wonder she was never around. Jasmine had really left him because she feared for her life! And Amber went out of town with him alone!

Amber had only seen one case of multiple personality disorder. It was almost too weird for her to believe. She had once worked with a client who believed she had 23 different personalities. The woman had been sexually and physically abused as a child. Amber remembered some of her personalities were men, and some were violent.

This woman had one personality she referred to as "S". She learned to use "S" to control the 22 other personalities. The personalities would all fight, finally with "S" winning over the others by overpowering them and throwing them all in an imaginary room, chaining the door.

Jasmine went on for awhile. She was obviously having her revenge by just spilling all the beans, watching the turmoil and disappointment on Amber's face.

Amber did not try to leave; it was Jasmine who finally dismissed her.

"Did you need anything else?" Jasmine stood; her slender hands were on her hips again, rolling her eyes when Amber didn't answer.

"I will let you let yourself out then."

"Just one question, Jasmine. How did the cops find him?"

The way Jasmine held her lips told Amber there might be fangs behind her smile.

"I told them where to go."

# 34

AMBER WAS STANDING outside her apartment and didn't remember how she got there. It all served her right! How could she let this happen? She stood outside her door, taking extra time before she realized there was a note tacked to her door. It was in Che's lopsided scrawl.

> Amber,
> *I have been trying to reach you to let you know that you have to get yourself over to Seton. Malik is having emergency surgery today and he was asking for you.*
>
> -Che.

What now? David momentarily left her thoughts as she ran to her car and drove to Seton Hospital. Her thoughts were racing as she entered the hospital, remembering she had ignored a call from Seton a day or so ago. An orderly pointed her to the information desk.

"I am looking for Malik Voyson, please. Do you know where he is?"

The volunteer at the desk ruffled through papers for what seemed like an eternity. Amber shifted her weight back and forth, realizing she needed to go to the bathroom.

"Okay," the clerk said. "Voyson? I think he must be in surgery still."

Amber walked away quickly, without thanking the man. What could have happened? Malik's voice was still on her answering machine, inviting her to listen to jazz. He was hoping he could help her tastes in music "grow up", as he put it.

She just didn't want to go with him, and now she felt bad. That might have been her last chance to hang out with him.

Amber realized how important Malik had become to her as she reviewed his phone message in her head. He was the only one of her friends whose motives Amber felt she never had to question. Maybe it wasn't too serious, she thought, but a feeling in the pit of her stomach told her otherwise.

It took her awhile to find someone who could fill her in. As she listened to what happened, she had flashbacks of her cousin.

"Mr. Voyson was shot in the face several nights ago while standing outside a nightclub. He's going to make it, but he has lost eyesight in both eyes. Thank God they used hunting pellets, or he might not be here at all."

Amber was stunned. Malik was the most honest and sincere person she knew. Why did it have to happen to him? How could someone just fire into a crowd of people? How many people were hurt, she wondered? Why was she just finding out? Her heart hurt thinking that he could have been gone, just like that. What would have happened if she had gone with him? She might be dead or something, too.

The doctor kept talking.

"Apparently the police have someone in custody. An ex-military guy, they say. What a shame. It will probably be in the paper. They picked this guy up for credit card fraud and embezzlement, and now they got him for attempted murder, too. They should put him *under* the jail. "

# Epilogue

DOCTORAL CANDIDATES always came last. She waited silently in the back of the auditorium with the other graduates. They listened anxiously for their cue to begin the procession.

As she waited, she could barely contain her excitement. In just a few hours, she would be Dr. Amber LaReaux, the first Ph.D. in her family. Amber thought about how proud her family was, especially her father who hadn't graduated from high school. His dream always was to have a doctor in the family, although he didn't say what kind of doctor. Amber was sure he didn't really get what her field was but that was okay.

Her entire family was waiting and watching. Amber knew

they would cheer loudly and make a scene when her name was called. Today, she could tolerate it. A few years ago, Amber would have tried to sink through the floor if her family embarrassed her as she knew they were about to do. But now, as she waited for the entry cue, she smiled. They had supported her, financially and otherwise, every crazy step of the way. She had come a long way. She was glad to have her family. Some of the other graduates didn't have anyone to cheer for them.

There was a time when she might not have gone to her graduation. That way no one would know about her family, where she was from or the things that happened to her. She still felt somewhat to blame for what happened to Malik. He didn't blame her though; he loved her, seemingly without limit.

Malik's surgery was partially successful. He had to wear glasses, but there were no permanent disfiguring marks. Four years later and Amber almost could not tell what happened. It was hard to believe he had used his GI bill money to pay for the surgery. Thank God for small miracles.

No matter how crazy David was supposed to have been, it was hard to believe that he was crazy enough to actually stalk Malik and shoot him. He even had the nerve to look Malik in the eye first. He was bothering other people too, going down the line on her phone bill and caller ID. He had been calling back numbers he didn't recognize and questioning people almost the entire time he had access to Amber's apartment.

Amber recalled that day she went to the hospital to see Malik as vividly as yesterday. She remembered listening to the doctor, realizing it was time for her to go. She knew she had to leave, to go home to Louisiana. She knew she was safe there, away from all the craziness that was around her. She was tired, but she now realized that she knew the dance because she, herself, created the steps. She had finally figured out what her grandmother said to her in her dreams was true. She let everything that happened to her come to pass, and it was time she changed the tempo and took control. She also knew then Che was just as bad as David. She really wasn't her friend at all. Sometimes you just have to let unhealthy things go, especially unhealthy relationships.

Che needed to stand on her own two feet and find motivation outside of Amber's life. She was a heavy weight and she had to go. She was getting too much pleasure from Amber's pain. Amber never spoke to her again. She ran into a church member in the mall right before she left for Louisiana and found out that Che had a drug problem that Amber hadn't known about. Che had been in rehab two times and eventually got married. Her husband became a minister and was now a Pastor at a large predominantly Black church in East Austin.

David went to the state psychiatric facility in Big Spring, Texas. Amber lost track of him after that, and she never saw Jasmine again. Amber knew David would like to think that he stole Amber from Tyler, crazy or not. He could not take the credit for that one. She alone had mustered up the courage to get out of her relationship with Tyler, although David had helped.

He had made her feel good, loved and beautiful when she needed it most, but that was the extent of it.

She sat by Malik's bed those first few days after the surgery, waiting for the doctors to remove the bandages. Amber was the first person he saw, albeit a little blurry. The minute she realized he could see, she realized she loved him. She could see him now, sitting in the auditorium with her family. He had even transferred to school in Louisiana to be with her, and they were getting married in two weeks.

More important than anything, Amber knew her past had made her what she was today. She was quite proud of that fact, and except for the Malik's shooting, she wouldn't change a thing.

# About The Author

Nina Foxx lives in Austin, Texas with her husband and daughter. She is originally from Jamaica, New York and she attended Hunter College as an undergraduate, and The City University of New York Graduate School for her graduate work, all in psychology. Her hobbies include ethnic dance, downhill skiing, and playing tennis in the afternoon.